Dearest
Mary Lou

Ann Cason

WESTBOW
PRESS®
A DIVISION OF THOMAS NELSON
& ZONDERVAN

This is a work of fiction. All of the characters, names, incidents, organizations, and dialogue in this novel are either the products of the author's imagination or are used fictitiously.

WestBow Press books may be ordered through booksellers or by contacting:

WestBow Press
A Division of Thomas Nelson & Zondervan
1663 Liberty Drive
Bloomington, IN 47403
www.westbowpress.com
1 (866) 928-1240

ISBN: 978-1-9736-8593-7 (sc)
ISBN: 978-1-9736-8592-0 (hc)
ISBN: 978-1-9736-8594-4 (e)

Library of Congress Control Number: 2020903125

Print information available on the last page.

WestBow Press rev. date: 02/20/2020

Contents

Preface

Many years ago, when I was much younger, I saw my mother pack in a box what appeared to be a stack of handwritten letters tied together with red ribbon. When I asked her about the letters, she paused what she was doing, looked out the window, and said one day she would tell me the story of the letters. My mother passed away in 2004, and the letters were packed for storage with her belongings. It has been many years since I first saw them. While unpacking boxes from a recent move to my new house, I discovered the letters still tied with the red ribbon. Thrilled at the discovery, I opened them and began to read how a beautiful love story grew out of the pain and anguish of World War II. It became apparent every generation is the same: needing and wanting to be loved and validated. I was so moved at their transparency that I simply had to share this love story.

Acknowledgments

I would like to say thank-you to some very special people in my life. Louise and Walter, your knowledge of the English language, the many hours you spent reading and rereading, and the wonderful time we shared together during this process will forever be remembered as a perfect example of unselfish love.

I am forever in debt to my dear friends Nita and Carolyn, who so delicately pointed out my errors and made suggestions that made this book a reality.

My dear Ashley, your frankness and direct approach to me helped me stay focused and realistic. Your unconditional love and support strengthened me to finish with confidence.

Madalynn and Emma, how do ones so young gain so much wisdom? Thank you for sharing your suggestions and comments. I am blessed to call you friends.

William, your supply of pictures, military resources, and suggestions helped me to organize my thoughts into a readable manuscript.

Paul, thank you for all the advice on the process of publication and encouragement to write from the heart.

My dearest Jim, how do I begin to ever repay you for your complete and total confidence in me to finish this project? Your encouragement kept me going after long days and nights at the computer.

It is my sincere hope and desire that all who read this will understand life is not without struggles, but perseverance will bring peace and joy. Never give up on your dreams!

Prologue

The Canterberry Hills Retirement Center was a beautiful place to live out her life. So many of her friends were living there also. The windows in her room faced the east, and the view was spectacular. Early each morning, Mary Lou would fix her coffee, settle down in her rocking chair, and watch the sun rise over Dolphin Cove Bay. As the warmth and light of the sun's rays filled her room, she remembered a time when love found its way into her life. The remnants of that discovery shaped every day of her life. She was once young and beautiful, but the years had gracefully replaced her soft, brown hair with hair as white as the sand on the beach where her true love for him had begun. Her daughter discovered the letters written to her during World War II and began asking questions. Explaining the tangled web of emotions among her, Luke, Bill, Ellie, and Flora would not be easy, so she answered her daughter's questions the best way she could: in a letter.

CHAPTER 1

She Remembers

It was the year 1943, and the war was claiming the young men to fight for freedom. A group of young men and women from the community known as Mossy Oak had grown up together sharing secrets, experiences, and discoveries of life. They were affectionately known as "the gang." The members of the gang were turning into serious-minded adults trying to find their way in a world of uncertainty. Because of the war and because the gang members were no longer children, the composition of this group was changing. Their lifeline to sanity was their connection to each other through letters. It became not a hobby but a way to hold onto what they knew as security.

Mary Lou was a beautiful young lady full of herself, was a bit precocious, and had a smile that made you want to give her anything she wanted. She was kindhearted, with a drive to be a little above the life she was given. Parties and dances were at the top of her list of fun things to do, and more often than not, she was the center of attention. She captured the heart of one member of the gang, Luke. Luke was a good-looking young man who chose to become a chaplain in the army. His gentleness with Mary Lou helped her through the rough years of the war.

Luke grew up in a Christian home and had the advantage of being the son of the pastor of Community Baptist Church. He was a quiet man yet stood strong and faithful in the face of temptation and difficulties of life. Luke was crazy about Mary Lou, and it was understood by the members of the gang they would one day marry. Luke joined the army as a chaplain, but not before he put an engagement ring on the hand of Mary Lou.

Bill, a rugged, handsome man, had a silver tongue with the ladies. A real sweet talker and a little dangerous for an innocent, inexperienced, young lady. Like the other young men in the gang, Bill took his place in the service to help with the war effort. His home life was somewhat dysfunctional. His parents divorced when he was very young, and his father remarried shortly thereafter. That experience set the stage for a search for acceptance and unconditional love.

He joined the army as a radio operator/navigator assigned to the 310th Bomb Group (M). Although Bill did not actually receive any time in the air confronting the enemy, being part of the communications personnel allowed him to be in the center of the activity. The ability to gather, evaluate, and distribute rumors became the number one diversion for all the soldiers and was considered a gift from the gods. Working in this department gave Bill the ability to construct these rumors such that they were taken as truth. The communication skills he developed during his enlistment would prove valuable later in his life.[1]

Flora, another member of the gang, was cute and petite. Her energetic and spontaneous personality captured Bill's heart. Flora kept Bill guessing about the level of commitment she was prepared to make with him. She could not make a total commitment but would not let him go to find the love he longed for.

Mary Lou and Bill began their correspondence when he entered the army. From day one, she kept this a secret for fear of losing Luke. Luke was a patient man but had his limits when it came to protecting his relationship with Mary Lou. She thought she loved Luke, but the more she corresponded with Bill, the more she realized something was missing in her relationship with Luke.

Bill was in the army to try to forget the love he had for Flora. He and Flora had grown up together in Mossy Oak. From a young age, they were pals, and as they grew older, their friendship turned to romance. They were constantly together. They attended Community Baptist Church and were members of the youth group. Most of the activities of the young people in the gang were sourced in this youth group. Cookouts, fishing, swimming, and baseball kept the gang together during those tender years of discovery. Happiness was Bill's until Franklin moved to the community—two houses down from Bill's home. He was the complete opposite of Bill, yet they became good friends.

Bill introduced Flora to Franklin, and she quickly became intrigued with him. After some time, she broke up with Bill and pursued a relationship with Franklin that led to their marriage. Bill thought possibly he had opened the door that allowed the love of his life to find the love of her life. He simply could not watch their relationship grow to a commitment of marriage. Flora knew she still had a place in Bill's heart and wanted to make sure it stayed there. She married Franklin on Bill's birthday.

The day of Bill's departure for basic training, Franklin and Flora were there to see him off, along with other members of the gang, including Mary Lou and Luke. Bill kissed Flora on the cheek and shook Franklin's hand. It was the best he could do; he was not capable of giving a verbal blessing to a relationship that changed the course of his life. He thought the farther he got away, the less it would hurt. He would discover that kind of hurt would never go away but could only be replaced with a greater love.

It was Mary Lou's day off, and she was taking it easy. The radio was on, and news of the fighting in the Mediterranean area was being discussed. She knew Bill was in that area and began to listen closely. The news report was not very specific for security reasons. There was no way for her to know the magnitude of the movements of just one squadron in the US Army Air Corps. The logistics of war were complicated, to say the least, but she listened to stay informed. After all, she had a lot invested in this war; her future was at stake.

Bill was a member of the 310th Bomb Group communications division. The 310th was ordered to Italy. The crews and operations personnel knew they were ordered to go but did not know to what part of Italy. Three missions were flown from the base at Menzel Temime before a severe rainstorm destroyed the landing fields and runways. The movement of the squadron was postponed until the entire squadron could be moved without disruption of missions.

While a small group proceeded to the base in Italy to prepare for the entire squadron's arrival, combat crews, accompanied by ground personnel to maintain twelve planes, went to Oudna Airfield near Tunisia. A total of nine missions were flown from that base. These missions were recorded in the daily log as the most accurate bombing skilled crews in the history of the squadron.

The majority of the squadron members were temporarily assigned to three different bases, Menzel Temime, Oudna A/D, and San Pancrazio, Italy. At the same time, a representative group for the 310th proceeded to the base in Italy for the purpose of preparing it for operation and the arrival of the planes, equipment, and personnel. It was reported by those in charge of preparing the base for occupancy that the setup was wonderful. Buildings had running water, and there were even fireplaces in some of the office buildings. Although there was a shortage of food, the stores were well stocked with reasonably priced items and the people were friendly and hospitable.

In the month of October 1943, thirteen officers and fifteen enlisted men completed fifty combat missions and were transferred from the squadron with no plans for replacements. The move to Italy had been scheduled and postponed so many times that it was finally abandoned and the group preparing the base was recalled to Africa.

The condition of the planes was classified as "mission weary," along with the ground equipment and some of the personnel. The status of the 310th Group was in limbo. They were an experienced combat force with basically no combat personnel and very few serviceable planes stationed at bases that were out of range of the enemy. The men of the 310th waited for information that would inform them when and where they would relocate and what their mission would be.

The month of November 1943 brought new and challenging changes to the 310th Bomb Group. The 310th and all its squadrons were transferred to the Forty-Seventh Wing, Twelfth Fighter Command, Twelfth Air Force, and began operating from the airport at Philippeville, Algeria. New and more powerful, the B-25-G replaced the B-25-C. While new B-25-G crews were receiving tactical training, seasoned combat men and crews were transferred out to complete their missions and return home.[2]

Mary Lou could hear her mother praying softly in the kitchen as she prepared lunch. Her mother's strong faith and example of true Christian love and acceptance held the family together after the death of her father. An unexpected heart attack leading to his death sent Mary Lou and her mother down a path of financial uncertainty. Fortunately, her mother had excellent money management skills and had saved quite a little nest egg. It would not last long but allowed her time to find a job that could support them both.

Mary Lou knew if her dad had not died, he would understand how she felt about Luke and Bill. If someone looked up *daddy's little girl* in the dictionary, Mary Lou's picture would be there. Her dad did not spoil her. He just adored her!

She heard the postman deliver the mail and quickly made her way to the mailbox, hoping to find a letter from Bill. She could not forget the heart-wrenching scene of departure when Bill left for basic training. She could feel his hurt and wanted to wrap him in her arms where his love would be safe. Although she was engaged to Luke, she simply could not get Bill off her mind. Bill and Luke were good friends. They had many hours of conversation about life and the hereafter. Luke's training as a chaplain was founded in the knowledge shared by his father, who was the pastor of Community Baptist Church. He had a soothing way of explaining life and how to negotiate through the difficulties. That was one of the characteristics Mary Lou loved about Luke. She felt safe with him—at peace and content.

Letter writing had become a lifeline for the members of the gang. Letters were literally flying back and forth across the Atlantic Ocean, the Pacific Ocean, and remote places on this earth. Somehow the gang kept together. The letters shared among them were the glue that held the group together. Mary Lou began to anticipate the arrival of Bill's letters with much excitement, more so than Luke's letters. Every time she heard the postman, her heart skipped a beat because it was Bill's letters she was looking forward to reading. After the news report was over, she made her way to the mailbox, and there it was.

October 18, 1943

Dearest Mary Lou,

Just received your letter and I sure was glad to hear from you and specially to know everything is Okay at home. Your letter was the first I have had in quite a while and it sure was cheerful too.

I'm glad you liked the picture I sent. I didn't expect the picture to be any good under the present conditions, but they came out better than I thought. I had hoped that I would get a picture of you in the letter you wrote but no pictures, that's OK do send me one when you can. I sure would like to see your picture. It sure has been a long time since I have seen any of the old faces, in fact so long I have almost forgot how you all look. You know I never realized it but in a few days, I will be celebrating my first year overseas. One year, that sure does seem like a long time. Before I go any further, I had better explain about the other half of this letter. The fellow's name is Rick, and I will have to say that he is the best fellow on the base. Every minute of the day I'm laughing at him. Just some of the crazy things he does makes anyone laugh. The other day he came along in broad daylight with a flashlight, so he goes over to a bag of drinking water and tells the guy next to it to hold the light for him. The guy shined the light for him and then started shouting for a dollar. Just things like that is what makes Rick. He does all them on purpose to make the boys laugh. If it wasn't for him some of us would go nuts and I'm not kidding. What he just wrote you in this letter is nothing new. You should hear what he tells me to my face and what he writes about me to his wife. I sure would like for you to drop him a line when you answer this letter because he doesn't get much mail, not much more than about 28 letters a week. Write him something that I can get a laugh on him. He writes letters like that all the time and he enjoys getting them the same way. I read a letter he got from a girl that works with his wife and she called him everything but

Ann Cason

a gentleman. He is a gentleman if I have ever saw one, but we get so much fun out of letters he gets like that. So much for that.

I will celebrate my anniversary the second of November, just 14 days before my birthday but 14 days from Flora's wedding. I was in tough shape to when she was married, and I only hope the world is at ease when I take that fatal step. No one in a struggle and none of our boys being killed is the way I want things to be and I feel sure they will be that way to. Things have been tough for everybody in this war. The boys that have wives and are over here sure take a beating.

Well this letter is getting a little long and out of my line, so I had better close. So, tell all the gang hello and I hope I will see you all before too much longer. Keep writing. Love, "Bill

October 18, 1943
AFRICA
Friday

Hello Mary-Lou,

You never heard of me I guess but that won't stop me from dropping you a gentle hint. It is about this fellow Bill. I know that you write to him because he tells me and besides, I see the return address on the envelopes. Look Mary, no doubt you don't know him very well or I know that you wouldn't be writing to him. He isn't worth the room he takes up and I should know because he not only works with me, he lives with me. All he does is talk about you and say how it is going to be between the two of you when he gets back. He just moons around all day and at night when he talks in his sleep, he mentions your name time after time. Is he in love I ask?? He must be. He is talking of cottages with a fence around it to keep the children from running into the street, flowers growing all around the place and you standing in the door waiting for him to come home.

You can't like him because he is good-looking because he was voted the most repulsive boy in the whole of north Africa. You can't like him because he has money because he is in debt to every soldier that is in the outfit. You can't like him because he has a gentle voice because he sings like a cow with a sore throat. What is it you see about him I don't know?

He makes a very poor soldier and can't do a thing in the right way. The other two fellows and I are always looking after him and if we didn't lead him around by the hand he would have gotten lost many, many, times.

He is sitting next to me right now, but he doesn't know that this is being written to you. I guess the reason is because he can't read very well. I think he gets the Chaplin to read his mail to him. Who writes his letters for him I don't know!

I have had some bad luck in this young life of mine, I have fallen out of trees, I have had toothaches, I have been shipped to Africa, but I never had any such as tough as that I am having now. Why did I have to get connected up with a guy like that??? I have tried several times to trade him off to the Arabs for some eggs, but they keep him for about two days and then they come around and offer me about twice as many eggs to take him back.

Can you suggest a way in which we can leave him here in Africa when we pull out? Maybe you don't realize it but if it hadn't been for him the Italians would have surrendered long ago and we would have been in Germany by now. You see, they see a guy like him in our Army and they figure if the rest of the Army is like him, we can't win.

Why the Army took him I don't know. maybe it was so we could look at him and get a good laugh. We need a good laugh once in a while to keep up our morale.

I pity the poor woman that falls in love with him. He is like a growing dog—always falling over himself and getting in everyone's way. I'm thinking of writing to Emily Post and asking her advice, but I thought I would write to you first and see if you had any suggestions. He is a mess, but I guess that you know that already and I needn't tell you.

I am going to let him finish this letter so what you read from here on out I don't know what it will be.

No doubt Bill is going to deny everything I have written but you may be sure that the part that I wrote is the truth. If you don't believe the things that I have written, you can write anyone in the outfit and they will back me up.

Be seeing you Mary-Lou, keep writing to Bill because letters mean a lot over here. Hope you know I am just teasing about Bill. He really is a great guy.

Your friend (I hope)

She folded the letters neatly and returned them to the envelope. How was she to understand what Rick was telling her about Bill? Surely, he could not be thinking anything like a serious relationship with her. They were part of the gang, but she was promised to Luke. Bill had seen the engagement ring Luke gave her. Although her interest in a relationship with Bill was growing, she knew she was no match for the other ladies he knew, including one in particular: Flora.

Her mom placed her lunch on the table, picked up the letters, and began to read what she felt in her heart was going to come between Mary Lou and Luke. Luke's father was the pastor of the church they attended. Their family was well respected in the community, and she knew Luke loved Mary Lou and would provide a stable and loving home for her. She also knew Mary Lou loved the attention from other suitors and she was young and wanted to act young. When Mary Lou's father passed away, it was Luke's family who offered a future of security for her. As she read the letters from Bill and Rick, she prayed for her daughter to be protected from any decisions that would draw her away from Luke.

While finishing her lunch, Mary Lou began thinking about removing her engagement ring. She knew this would create questions she was not prepared to answer but decided to remove it anyway. She gently slipped her engagement ring into the pocket of her dress. She hoped her mother would not notice. Her mother's firm expression gripped her heart when she left the kitchen. She wanted her mother's approval in every phase of her life. However, the commitment of marriage to Luke was her decision and she would make the right decision for her, even if she had to stand alone without her mother's support and approval.

Chapter 2

Flora's Double

The United States entered WWII on December 7, 1941, when the Japanese bombed Pearl Harbor. The Second World War became the biggest war in the history of humankind. Only a few countries were not involved in the fighting that destroyed large areas of Europe and the Far East. This war changed the dynamics of the American family and brought on an explosion of music and movies to encourage support for the boys fighting for freedom.

The big band era was in full swing, and dance bands like Tommy Dorsey, Duke Ellington, Louis Armstrong, and Benny Goodman played swing music for those left behind, the servicemen stationed in the US, and those on furlough. Dance halls opened in almost every town. GIs and locals would go there to dance, and many were caught up in the romance of the war and married a hope and dream in their dance partner. The Mills Brothers had the number one song for October 1943, "Paper Doll," and Harry James, Bing Crosby, and Frank Sinatra dominated the music industry with their smooth ballads of love.

Mary Lou loved to dance. Every Friday night, she and some of the gang would go to the dance hall in Pine Terrace, a little community across the bay from Mossy Oak. Mary Lou's mother hoped that by seeing different men and how they treated women, she would reach the conclusion what she had in her relationship with Luke would be a Christian marriage. That meant a strong and stable foundation. All dolled up in a slightly form-fitting, midcalf, light-blue dress with a wide satin belt, she would dance every dance until the doors closed.

Mary Lou knew her mother did not approve of her decision to remove her engagement ring, but she also knew she could not deny the feelings she was developing for Bill. Dancing helped her keep her mind occupied and her feelings under control until she could sort them out. But what could she do about Flora? Flora's memory was buried deep in Bill's heart, and she left him with a reminder he would carry forever. Mary Lou was at a loss to resolve the relationship between Flora and Bill but kept her fears to herself.

December 29, 1943

Dearest Mary Lou,

Just a couple lines to say hello and that I'm still thinking about you. How did you spend Christmas? I bet you had a good time. Wish I could have been there to help you celebrate. Mary Lou, please excuse this writing. I'm a little tired I just got back from the hospital and I have been driving almost all day. Remember me telling you about Rick, well I brought him home today, he sure was glad to get home too. He said he would write you a line as soon as he had time although I can't see where he is so busy, what a guy.

I had a picture made the other day and I sent you one in this letter. It was made with a small camera and you almost have to have a magnifying glass to see me but it's a picture anyway. You didn't show my picture to Flora, did you? I hope not I don't know what the idea is, but someone sent me a few pictures of Flora the other day. It sure did me good to see her again but I don't know who sent them, you didn't did you? The letter I got didn't have a return address on it and I couldn't tell by the handwriting. If anyone mentions it to you tell them thanks for me, will you.

Well things are about the same as ever over here. I talked to a couple of American nurses this morning and it sure was good to hear an American girl talk again. That is the second American girl I have spoken to in the last

14 months, pretty long time, isn't it. You remember last November when we came in to Casablanca, I don't know exactly know how to tell you but anyway we went from Casablanca to a place called "Lavis Gentil," the place had a few people left among the ruins and after a couple days there I walked past a girl I do believe was Flora's double I had to look twice to satisfy myself that it wasn't her. I know she couldn't understand English and when I spoke to her all she said was "No com pree" meaning she didn't understand but if she had said hello Bill I would have passed out, it would have killed me. She was dressed in nothing but rags and had no shoes. When I asked her about her clothes she said, "fini" or "finish." Meaning that was all she had. I'll tell you I never felt so sorry for anyone in my life and I'll say again she was beautiful so I reached for my bank roll which was pretty large at that time and I bought her a complete outfit from head to foot, cost me about twenty five dollars but that is money well spent and went to a good purpose. I never did see her after that because we moved out the next day, but since then I have been thinking about her, the way she looked when I first saw her and the way she looked when I bought her some clothes. It left a picture in my mind that I'll never forget. I still think if she and Flora were side by side you couldn't tell them apart. Of course, I haven't seen Flora for a long time, but she looked just exactly the way Flora did when I left for this country. I'm sure glad the people at home don't have to go through the things that these people are going through.

Well, well what do you know, I received a Christmas card from Flora. That is the only word I have heard from her in 14 months. I was glad to hear from her. She asked me to drop her a line once in a while, but she never put her address on the envelope, so I don't know where to write. Does she still live with her people? If you will do me a favor I sure will appreciate it, give her a letter for me, I'll put it in this letter. The next time you see her you can give it to her.

Well Mary Lou, I guess all I can say for myself is that I'm feeling fine, in the best of health and want to get back just as bad as ever, also I had a very swell Christmas — tell you about New Years later. So, for now I'll just say so long and write very soon. Lots of Love "Bill"

Bill continued to hang onto the memory of his true love, Flora. She didn't make it easy for him to let go when she sent him Christmas cards and requested that he write to her. He was having trouble with writing to her. What did you say to your ex-girlfriend when she was married to one of your good friends? Even more difficult was the ability to maintain an emotional state that allowed for good judgment during war times while trying to mend a broken heart.

Jan 9, 1944

Dearest Mary Lou,

Well here I am once more, and I do hope you are feeling fine. How are all the folks at home, not working too hard are they, hope not anyway.

Everything with me is about the same, they still keep us on the go most of the time. Right now, I'm listening to the radio, we get some good music once in a while from London, England. The only trouble with the London station is that they are about two or three years behind in music. Some of the songs I heard before I came into the Army are just now becoming popular with them, but it beats nothing anyway. Have you been doing much bowling since you wrote last? We saw a picture show in the hanger the other day and it seems that bowling is becoming very popular since the war started. Everyone plays it. It showed some the factory recreation centers back home and said they were always crowded. I bet it's just about that way at home also, and another game that is coming into play and that is pool. All the USO centers all seem to have them. You know I just thought about something, it seemed awful funny that when I was home on furlough there wasn't many soldiers or sailors on the streets like there was before I came in the Army. What happened to them all, is Dolphin Cove off limits or something? I never thought about it until just now, I've been thinking about the few last days at home. My furlough could have been better, I just seem to get the wrong breaks that's all. I'll be home again soon though and I have a feeling things are going to be right this time. Rick said tell you hello and he also said tell you now that he has shaved and combed his hair you should know which is the better looking. What a guy. I've never seen another like him yet. He and I just got back from a hike in the mountains and the moon was so full and bright, I just couldn't help from thinking— just thinking—of course now if I were home I might get someone else to take a moon light walk with. I don't think his pictures did him justice. He is a much better looking guy than his pictures and the main thing is he hasn't an enemy in the world, that is with the exception of the fellows we are fighting. I think a lot of him. I think I sent you a picture of him, didn't I? Speaking of pictures did you receive the one I sent a few days ago? I'll say that wasn't much of a picture. I'll try to do better next time. Every time I look at your picture you seem to get prettier, I wouldn't take a fortune for it.

Well I guess I had better close for this time, it's getting a little late so for now I'll just say write soon and a very good night to you,

Love, Bill"

As Mary Lou tucked his letter into a secret place in her bureau, she thought about a moonlight walk on the beach they both loved so much. She was falling deeper in love with him after each letter.

January 28, 1944

Dearest Mary Lou,

Just a line to say hello and to tell you I'm still in the best of health and all that stuff. How have you been since I wrote you the last time, still not working too hard, I hope. I had a letter from the folks a few days ago and they said that all the old gang was home for the Christmas holidays, did you get to see them? They said all the guys sure did look good. They said some had gained weight and others had lost weight. You know, I think the service builds a fellow up, well that is in some ways it does, but it seems to build all of them up in body. The folks say all the boys look good. Those boys are seeing quite a bit of the world these days. That will be something to tell their grandchildren of the places that they have been and seen, that is going to be something.

Rick said he was going to write you today and give it to me but I see that he has an envelope with your address on it so he is going to mail it. I guess he didn't want me to read it but I don't think I have to because I can just about tell what is in it. I bet he sure handed you a line about me didn't he? But he is a good guy and I think lots of him, he is almost like a brother to me. Well that is in some ways. I can't see yet where he finds enough to talk about. He sits down every night and writes his wife a six- page letter and she does the same. I asked him once what did he talk about, what did he tell his wife about this place that he could fill up six pages of typing and he said that he wrote a page of nothing, but that he is still in good health and all that sort of stuff and the other five he would write how much he loves her. That guy sure is crazy about his wife, he is next to me now writing her. I think I told you about him being in the hospital some time ago, didn't I? He has been out now for quite some time but he still has to watch his diet, he isn't supposed to eat anything with grease in it. He seems to be ok now, but his eyes were yellow for a while after he got out of the place up there, I mean the hospital. The way that I met him was over a good dinner, which at the time, was something of a novel thing to get because food was something that was hard to get. We got out one afternoon and bought a few chickens and had them fried up real nice with fried potatoes and all the trimmings and had the boys over for dinner and he was in the group. What a good time we had at that little dinner party. I have never laughed so much in my life at any one guy. He kept up such a line of nonsense that you couldn't help for laughing. From that time on I have been with him and he is still the same way as he was the first time I saw him, the same old guy and just as funny as ever. He said that he was going to teach me how to train a wife (if I ever get one).

Well I guess I can't write much tonight I seem to make too many mistakes an on top of that I can't seem to think of anything to say except that I think of you and hope to see you in the near future. Write when you can, and I will do the same I have to close for now. Good night.

Love, "Bill"

CHAPTER 3
Boys in the Army

January 28, 1944
Friday
12:35 Noon

Hello Mary Lou,

This won't be too much of a letter because I just wrote a five page letter to my wife so I guess I am not in much of a letter writing mood. Another thing, I am deeply in love with my wife and she with me so I write things to her that get me thinking along lines of love and then when it comes time to write to another person I am apt to have her on my mind and I do a poor job. I'll try my best to make it a good letter and I will try to keep from mentioning my darling wife, too often.

It has been quite some time since I wrote to you last and I am rather ashamed of myself but a lot has taken place since I wrote the last time. Among them was a trip that I took to the hospital for four weeks, I suppose that Bill told you. I had a case of yellow jaundice and I had to go on a diet and the boys here at the base couldn't feed me the way I had to be so off I went. It sure is a surprise to me how much I missed Bill while I was in the hospital but I really did. eme to see me a few times and I sure looked forward to those visits then when I came back here to the bunch, it was just like coming home again. I don't guess that I have to tell you what a nice fellow Bill is because, after all, you have known him a lot longer than I but I doubt if you knew him as well as I do. He is a grand person and I think a lot of him. I know that he has made a big change since you last saw him and you will hardly know him but then again, you have changed too and when he sees you again I know that he is in for a bit of a surprise. It is about a year and a half since you and he saw each other and let me tell you, a lot can and does happen to people your age.. You two are full grown adults and how you have turned out in the past two years is apt to be the way you are going to be for the rest of your lives. That's no kidding either.

Bill is taller than he was, he is heavier and I think he is better looking than when I first knew him. This Bill lad is a good looking boy and I don't mean maybe. I have done my best to see to it that he doesn't pick up any bad habits while he is in the Army and I think I'm doing a pretty good job. He has never had a date since he is over seas and he doesn't drink at all. He won't gamble and he doesn't curse anymore. I don't mean that he is a goodie-goodie or a sissy because if I said that I would include myself because I don't do any of those things either and I know that Bill and I can take care of ourselves very well.

Well enough of Bill for the moment. I am interested in you. Tell me, are you going to break his heart? Bill thinks a lot of you and if you ask me, you are his best girl. In fact, I think you are his only girl. He has the picture that you sent to him right next to his bed and every morning when he wakes up he says, "good morning sweetheart" and every night before he goes to sleep he says, "Goodnight, darling" to your picture so I have reached the conclusion that he is sort of that way about a certain person. I think he has ideas of making that last name of hers exactly like his. Do you remember the girl that broke his heart? Well, he has just about gotten over that and I have convinced him that she wasn't the right girl for him. I haven't done any coaching about you, in fact, I sort of run you down a little just to hear him brag about you and how nice you are. Remember even if I am sort of talking about you it is only in fun and to get a rise out of him. I think, from what he has told me about you, that you are tops and I know I would like to meet you. I received the letter that you sent to me and from the moment that I read it I thought a lot of you because you knew I was married and you were afraid that if my wife found out that I was writing to another girl she might get mad. That really sold me on you because most girls don't stop to think about things like that. It showed me you have a good head on your shoulders and you didn't want to come between any couple.

Mary Lou, my wife knows me pretty well and she knows just how much she means to me. She trusts me and she knows that she will always be able to trust me so if I write to other girls she never worries about it. I feel the same way about her and if we couldn't trust each other we would never had married, so, don't you worry about that anymore.

In my last letter to you I sort of teased you about Bill but I am glad that you know it was only teasing. You know how fellows are so I know you didn't take me seriously.

I was going to let Bill put this in with his letter to you but I don't want him to read it so I'll put it in an envelope by itself an he won't know what is in it. You don't have to answer this if you don't wish to but I hope that you will. If you haven't the time or the inclination just mention in one of your letters to Bill that you got it. Please excuse the mistakes I have made, but you see, this is a young typewriter and it doesn't know how to spell as yet.

This is about all that I can think of at this moment so I will close now. Keep writing to Bill because it sure keeps his morale up and I like him happy. Stay well and we'll try to get home soon.

Your friend and Bills (I hope) Rick

Ann Cason

Mary Lou was writing more to Bill than to Rick. Maybe it was her inexperience with male relationships, or maybe it was a bad joke, but she simply did not know what to believe about Bill.

Rick's first letter ran him down, and his second letter built him up. Now Bill wanted to know what Rick said about himself. They were acting like they had in high school as teenagers. Weren't they supposed to be fighting a war?

She needed and wanted to talk with Luke, but he was just as far away as Bill. On her nightstand was a little jewelry box Luke had given her. She opened the box, retrieved the ring, and placed it halfway on her ring finger. *Maybe I was wrong,* she thought. *Maybe I was wrong.*

CHAPTER 4

Luke

Luke came home on leave for some much-needed R&R. With so much death and destruction around the soldiers in the war, he was emotionally worn out counseling and trying to give answers to questions that had no answers. Mary Lou returned the engagement ring to her finger. She did not have the heart to break his heart. It was good to see him again because he brought a sense of normalcy to her life, including a peace and contentment. He was quiet and safe.

He was home for two weeks, and they spent every day together. Luke took her to and from work and to dinner. He made sure her limited time with him was pleasant, and any requests she made he tried to fulfill. But he could sense there was a strange distance between them. She was not herself. He knew she was writing to several of the soldiers and wondered if Bill was one of them. He was curious because Bill was writing to him. Bill was a little on the free-spirited side and crazy about Flora. He simply did not understand how Mary Lou could even consider him as husband material. The day Luke returned to his outfit overseas, he kissed her goodbye. The magic was gone. He feared she was lost to a phantom soldier.

Mary Lou continued to wear the ring, partly because she felt guilty for not honoring her commitment to Luke, and it was a safe way to not get involved with the fellows seeking her attention. She wrestled with her feelings toward Bill. Did he really care for her, or were his words just those of a homesick soldier? Was she just the outlet for him to vent his frustrations, dreams, and hopes? She was in uncharted territory with her feelings, yet she continued to write to him. Rick was another issue. She knew Bill and Rick were best buddies, but she could not figure out his motive for writing the stuff he wrote about Bill's credentials and feelings for her. He obviously did not know about Ellie.

Because the composition of the gang moved into the written word, Mary Lou had to be very careful what she wrote and to whom. She knew Bill was writing to several members of the gang, but was he sharing with them what she wrote to him? She wrote to Luke and explained to him she needed a little time to think about her future. The war brought so many changes, not only material but also emotional. She tried to explain it would be best if they could resolve this after the war was over and he returned home. He agreed, and that seemed to ease the tension between them. Luke, however, was not so optimistic, yet he continued to hope she made the right choice: him! Time would tell!

Her mother was pleased she was wearing the ring again. It was a symbol to her she was back on course. Mary Lou did not discourage that line of thinking; it bought her some time and relief from judgment.

CHAPTER 5
The 310th Bomb Group

In the words of Brigadier General Robert D. Knapp,

> When the complete history of the American Twelfth Air Force is written, one B-25 Mitchell bombardment group will certainly share top honors. This group is 310th. In thirty months of intensive combat operations in the Mediterranean theater, from Casablanca to Northern Italy, the final count is an amazing record for a single group to have achieved.
>
> - a total of 989 missions flown
> - more than 17000 sorties flown
> - more than 23,000 tons of bombs dropped
> - more than 400 enemy aircraft destroyed
>
> Operating from Maison Blanche in Algeria, on December 2, 1942, eight B-25s took part in a bombing raid in the area of the Gabes Airdrome in Tunisia. Under the command of Colonel Anthony G. Hunter of Kansas City, Missouri, began a series of raids by these Mitchell bombers against vital targets in all parts of the Mediterranean theater. Several of these early fliers were veterans of the Doolittle raid on Tokyo. In the Battle of the Kasserine Pass, a German counteroffensive in

the struggle for North Africa, B-25s of the 310th were given the call for close aerial support to the ground troops. Experimenting with tactics later evolved into a devastating system, the 310th bombed the Germans close to our lines with such effectiveness as to be instrumental in their withdrawal.

After Tunisia, the 310th concentrated its destruction upon small well-fortified islands of Pantellaria and Lampedusa, and it was air power alone that forced the Italians to surrender those bastions.

June 1943 found the 310th assuming a role it was to play more than any other in the war: the bombing of enemy communications. During the attacks in the Rome area, the invasion of Sicily, the Salerno fight, the Anzio beachhead, and the drive on Cassino, the 310th was at work destroying bridges, railroad passes, viaducts, and marshalling yards. All means that the Germans employed to transport men and supplies to their front were hit by the 310th.

The Northern Italian campaign helped bring about the German collapse by flying close aerial support to the Fifth and Eighth armies in their final drive. First from Corsica, then from its new base in Italy, the group was fighting the Battle of the Srenner Pass, which kept the route blocked from January 28, 1944, until the end of the war. While the Germans were escaping across the River Po, B-25s bombed enemy equipment areas and ferry and platoon staging areas.

On its last mission, the 310th Bomb Group said goodbye to the Germans by dropping leaflets instead of bombs— leaflets announcing the unconditional surrender of the German High Command in Italy.[3]

Bill grew up really fast when he joined the army and was assigned to the 310th Bomb Group. His eyes were opened to life's truths. Love and hate had no defined boundaries, and friendships and family were the glue that held life together. He discovered sleep didn't come easily. The sound of bombs exploding, buildings crumbling, and people screaming invaded his thoughts. The experience, shared by one of the fighter pilots, of firing on another aircraft and watching the enemy pilot's face reflect unspeakable terror would prevent him from closing his eyes. Still fresh in his mind were the voices of the pilots who flew a recent mission to destroy a German communications and supply depot only to discover friendly Allied forces were on the ground. They came close to destroying their own.

BooBoo1030, Charlie24, and Devildog14 were US pilots assigned to this unit. They were obviously shaken up by this experience and began to review the mission in detail to try to understand what went wrong. BooBoo1030, a young pilot, was operating under intelligence given that no friendlies were in the area, and his visual sightings of what appeared to be rocket launchers were the targets they were to destroy. He was ready to drop his load. Charlie24, a seasoned combat pilot, had learned the hard way to take a second look before destroying life and property. He saw markers on the targets that could be friendly. He knew the value of a second look and proceeded to make another pass to be sure. DevilDog12, also a seasoned combat pilot, encouraged BooBoo1030 to hold off until they could determine what the markings were.

As Bill listened to their conversation, he could feel their sense of relief as they described what they saw as Allied forces. Killing another human was life altering, even if he was the enemy. But to kill your own was more than they could bear.

He remembered how another buddy described his role as a gunner in a dogfight between their B-25 and enemy aircraft.

> Enemy planes all around us. Our plane was full of bullet holes. The sound of bullets tearing through the steel frame was deafening. I looked down and realized I was shot in the leg but had no time to deal with it. I continued to shoot and holding that fifty-caliber machine gun was

like holding a team of wild horses out of control. I hit two of my targets and cleared a way for our pilot to find the way back to the base. All the while, the faces of those I love flashed through my mind.

He could only imagine the terror his buddy felt. Bill wondered if he himself were wounded, would he have a chance to tell his loved ones how much he loved them? Would he have a chance to ask them to forgive him if he hurt them? He softly said to himself, "Mary Lou, Flora, Ellie, please don't give up on me."

His letters might seem redundant and boring talking about the same things, but it was the conversation that kept him sane. The connection to the reality of people and places that represented strength and security was his lifeline to joy in a world of destruction. So he took pen and paper in hand and wrote, "Dearest Mary Lou ..."

CHAPTER 6

First Date

Corsica

Feb 15, 1944

Dearest Mary Lou,

I received your very sweet letter today and enjoyed hearing from you as much. How are things around home these days, just fine I hope. Things around here haven't been too hot for some time, in fact it has been cold as everything here. The snow up on the mountain sure is pretty. I've been thinking of going up there but I'll have to get a few more clothes first.

I got a letter from one of the guys in the gang the other day. He said he was back from a furlough and did not get a chance to visit with you. He said he was sorry that he didn't get to see you, but he was too busy. Can you guess who it was? He said he did see you beside the road one morning but didn't have time to talk to you so he waved to you but realized you did not recognize him. He also said you were just as pretty as ever. From the way he talked about the old community there isn't much left there. I never could picture that place as being dead, there was always too much excitement among the boys and girls. I guess now that most of the boys have left and the girls have married things did quiet down somewhat. The folks said if I could come home I wouldn't know the place, is that right? Has it changed that much? Everything may be changed but from your letters you are still just as sweet as you always were and if you will pardon my boldness, I don't think you could change if you wanted to, you will always be the same to me. Instead of people moving into Mossy Oak, I hear someone is moving out. What war will do to a place, prices go up and people start moving around. No one seems to be settled any more, everyone seems to be seeking excitement. I wish those people could come over here and let me go home. When I got over here everything was new and I liked it but that seems to be something of the past now. Well I know I'll get to come home some day and what a day that's going to be. When this war is over, and everything has quieted down somewhat I'm gonna settle down and never leave that place. I think I've seen enough of the world and had enough excitement to last me the rest of my life. Of course, I think now things won't be what they use to and I'll have to reacquaint myself with the new changes and get to know things as they happen. I think the old place around home would look even better to me right now than it did before I left. When I left Mossy Oak things seem to be in full swing. Everything that has happened at home and all the changes that have taken place, I have just heard about it I haven't seen any of it.

I'm sure glad to hear that you and Luke have made up. I don't like to see you mad at anyone. I've seen too much of this breaking up and all that sort of stuff and the thing that gets me now in regard to my situation, is that it was all my fault. Now is no time to cry over spilt milk, I think I've changed since those days. Another reason I'm glad you and Luke are friends again is that if he did come overseas writing to each other and making up would never be like seeing each other. I had rather see the person, and I can assure you that it did Luke good. Well I've just got back from chow so I'll write another couple of lines if I can think of anything to say. To start with, Rick said tell you hello and all that sort of stuff. That Rick is a great guy and I don't know what I would do without him. When things seem pretty low and everyone is ready to snap your head off he always comes through with something to put the boys in better spirits. I don't think I could be in a better spirit I just got your letter and a very sweet letter it was too.

In your letter you spoke about going bowling and you said you sure would be glad when I can be home to go with you all. What do you mean by "go with you all?" Who all is going be in that party? I think I know what you mean, that there is going to be another couple along —right or is there gonna be a couple of boys besides myself. You know that brings us back to what I was saying some time ago. Suppose all the boys come home at once and they all wanted the first date with you, what then? Boy oh boy I don't want to miss that. It all comes down to what I was told once before, "may the best man win" and I'm sure the best man will win too. On the first date business I can see where I'm going have plenty of competition because all the fellows are looking forward to that day. What are some of the best places in Dolphin Cove to enjoy a nice dinner and then some dancing? Never mind the prices, I've got that covered., Just the best is what I want for you. It has been so long since I've seen that place around there I'm afraid I would get lost. When I was stationed in the States I got home once and I thought I would never find my way around. People would mention places to me and I wouldn't even know where it was although I had been there before I left home. That's just how being away from home so long will affect you. Oh yes I got a book the other day and looked up Dolphin Cove, it told about things that I have never heard about. The names of places have changed, and new places have come up that I'm afraid I wouldn't even know the place. One thing though if you ever want to come over here after the war you need me as a guide. I can just about take you through any of these countries blind folded I don't think I can get lost over here.

I sure hope you had a happy birthday and I sure hope Luke made it home to be with you, if he didn't maybe all of us will be home for your next one. Mary Lou if you don't mind my asking how old are you? When you write tell

Ann Cason

me if Luke did make it home, I'm very interested in you too very much. Did you and Luke break up before he went into the Army or after and that was the trouble. Don't tell me he was jealous, that's pretty bad I know I was that way once and it got me exactly nowhere. I'm sure it wasn't that because Luke is not that way. It must have been something else.

I wish those pictures you were talking about were here, I sure would like to see them. I can be sure they are good because they are you. The picture I sent you some time ago was made at Philippeville in Africa that sure was a rest camp. We were stationed near the city itself and had lots of fun and what do you know I even went to a dance there. Of course, the girls were French but it was good just to see a girl again. I think we stayed there for about three months or something like that. That was quite a place. The way it goes is that every time we move we can tell where we moved from but not where we moved to. I can tell you that I'm in Corsica but I can't say where, but I think you could very easily guess because this is not a big place like Africa.

I Don't know if that last paragraph will get through or not but I'll take a chance anyway.

Mary Lou it was this morning when I started this letter but I've had to write at odd times and in between my work. I was the "DSO" today which means Duty Signals Officer or something like that. Right at the moment it is 7:05 our time and 2:05 by your time, just six hours difference that's all. Things are a little cold outside, but the fellows have a good fire in here and it is nice and comfortable.

I thought I could think of some more things I wanted to tell you, but I guess I can't so I'll just close for this time. Write soon and I'll do the same. Love, "Bill"

As she read the letter, her hopes of finding a place in his heart were coming true. Maybe, just maybe, she would be able to help him let go of his love for Flora. She didn't see Flora very much because Flora was married and was struggling to hold onto that relationship. Bill did not know she was pregnant and now resided with her parents because they could not afford their home. He would know soon, however, because someone in this gang would write and tell him, but it would not be her.

Bill was trying desperately to move on with his life, but he was caught in a web of emotion when it came to Mary Lou. His admission of his romantic interest in her was clouded by his honor to not cut out Luke. He tried to clarify in his mind he was not the reason their relationship was failing. He was so homesick he simply could not let go of Mary Lou at this time. She was so faithful and kept the conversation light. She was honest with him regarding her dating/engagement status and never pushed him for a commitment. Bill admitted coming home would bring new challenges, both physical and emotional. His hometown was now a memory, and what he would come home to would be bits and pieces of that memory scattered throughout a town he once had known.

CHAPTER 7

New Home

The move to town was imminent. Life had been tough financially since the death of her father. Mary Lou lived with her mother, and the savings her mother had accumulated before her father died, along with her salary, was paying the bills, but it was not going to last very long. She was offered a promotion as supervisor in the accounts payable department, which would cover their living expenses and even leave a little left over. The move to town would put her closer to her job, and she could walk to work and save the bus fare. The downside to the move was it would place her farther away from where Bill would live when he came home.

Bill's parents bought a sixty-acre farm about forty-five minutes north of Dolphin Cove. It had a creek that ran through the middle of the property and fed a large lake stocked with a variety of fish. His family farmed the land and produced seasonal vegetables, along with raising cattle, pork, and poultry. There was no shortage of good country cooking at Bill's home. Most everything eaten was grown on the farm. Lots of jellies and jams were made from blueberries, strawberries, peaches, and pears, and spread onto one of those cathead biscuits was a joy you were not soon to forget. Fried chicken and barbecue were the best in the south. His home was in such a remote area that there was no indoor toilet; they used an outhouse. No telephone. The closest phone was at the general store three miles away, and there was no power. That meant cutting firewood for the woodstove and three fireplaces. Their backgrounds were very different. Mary Lou was a city girl, and Bill was a country boy. How could a union of two totally different backgrounds succeed without serious adjustments? Love was blind to those in love.

Luke's family helped move what furniture and belongings they had. They were always there to help in any situation. So why could she not see the blessings of a marriage into that family? From his letters, Luke appeared to accept the "wait and see" decision about their relationship and future. In the meantime, he showered her with gifts from Europe. French porcelain dinnerware, a sixty-five-piece set of Lenox flatware, a diamond bracelet, and enough clothing to fill her closet. Money was no object. Dedication, loyalty, financial stability, and a Christian foundation belonged to him, but something was missing. She knew the day would come when she would have to decide, but not now. She could tell from Bill's letters his heart was softening toward her. He was curious about her status with Luke and their long-term commitment. Did that mean she had a chance? She knew he was writing to Ellie, the sister of his friend Troy, so she held her heart in check and kept writing.

19 February 1944

Somewhere in Corsica

Dearest Mary Lou,

Received your letter the other day and I do hope you will excuse me this time for not answering any sooner, but I just haven't had time. Things have been pretty busy around here the last few days although I did get a chance to write you a letter the day before yesterday. I got the second letter from you the same day that I wrote that one. I spoke of the long one because I don't usually write a letter that long, but I guess I just happened to be in the mood for writing letters that day. I think I wrote one to everyone including Flora.

I don't think I told you, but I got a letter from her a couple of days ago and I was so surprised to hear from her. I thought she had forgot me completely. I guess she is a little lonesome now that her husband is gone and I don't know that I could blame her a bit because it is pretty bad to be away from the one you love, believe me I know I understand that she is living with her folks again and had to sell all their furniture, that is about the way it goes. One minute everything is going swell and everyone seems to be happy when the Army or Navy gets the idea that you could do better someplace else and the first thing you know you are out in the desert someplace away from your wife or husband. She said that her husband left just two weeks before Christmas, I bet she sure had a dull Christmas. That is the main thing in married life I couldn't imagine it would be very happy with him gone and what do you know she says that she is going to be a mother sometime in July, so she tells me. Why she tells me these things I don't know but she seems to be happy about it, so I'll let well enough alone. The fact that she is going to have a baby surprised me more than the letter because I was about half way expecting her to write but was not expecting to hear about the baby. Not only did she miss Christmas with her husband but she is going to miss him now more than ever. That sure is a tough break for her but she seems to be in good spirits and says that she can hardly wait. I don't know how I got on that subject but never-the-less there it is. I wouldn't say anything about it because I don't know that she wanted it too much around. Please don't mention it, it sure does make good writing material, doesn't it?.

I could write page after page about her and give her all sorts of good advice but the trouble with me is that I can't seem to follow my own advice, I'm always sticking my neck out for someone else and I never seem to get the advantage out of it oh well one of these days I'll let someone give me some good advice and then I'll get the good out of it. Someone gave me some good advice about a couple years ago but I was just like the rest of the guys my age, we said that it is a bunch of hot air. I don't know if you can follow me in this letter or not because I don't know that I can follow myself very much. It seems that I have a lot on my mind right at the moment, but I can't seem to put into words what I want to say. Maybe you can read between the lines and you can get a general idea of what I am trying to say. Sometimes I get to thinking about the times I use to have in the States and while I was home and all that sort of stuff and it seems to get to me. Maybe that is what is wrong with me now. Don't get me wrong, there is nothing physical wrong with me and if I can help it I don't think there will be but when I get to thinking about home and some of the crazy stunts that I pulled I could kick myself. I can sit here now and see just what I did that wasn't right and also see the things that I could have done that would have been right or put things right that were wrong right again. Sometimes I wonder just why I didn't do the things that were right. I guess everyone can see the mistakes that he or she makes after they have made them.

I think I got off the subject a little bit didn't I but I have to have something to talk about except that it is very cold at the present, I could say it is snowing but it isn't and anyway I don't think talking about the weather is a very good subject anyway. Some people such as the censor seem to think that is military information and I suppose it is I don't know, I can see very plainly how it would benefit the enemy because if you will look at the map of Corsica you will understand that we are covered by the enemy on all sides except one in other words this place is more north than most of them. We can't go much further without being in the German's hands and that isn't good is it. Say there is something that I have been wanting to ask you for some time, have you ever gotten a letter from me that has been cut up in anyway? I have been wondering if I have ever talked about anything that they would cut. Rick got a letter from his wife saying "I'm sure glad that you have a nice time in ___" the part that is blank is what the censor cut out. In one letter that he got from his wife she said that all she got was hello my darling and signed your husband Rick and all the rest of the letter was cut out. The trouble with that is he had made the letter that way, and he sure did get a laugh out of it to. When she got the letter and answered she said she was writing but didn't know what was in his letter to answer. Rick ask me a minute ago if he could

Ann Cason

write a couple lines in this letter, should I? I don't think you will mind will you? I can't seem to think of anything to write about maybe he can, well here he is anyway.

Well here I am, and it wasn't my idea. So-o-o-o, if I can't think of anything to write we will blame it on him. Of course, I don't' know what Bill wrote in the rest of this letter but I will assume that he told you that we are no longer in that forsaken land of north Africa. We are now in the fair land of Corsica and its sure beats that place we just left. There are mountains here and on the tops of them there is a lot of snow. That is something that Bill hardly ever saw before in his life, so he gets a thrill out of it. It is a lot colder here than it is in your neck of the woods and poor Bill almost freezes every night. I think that he will live till summer though and then perhaps we won't be in a cold country next winter. Perhaps, we will even be home and we will have our love to keep us warm. I will have my wife and Bill will have ____? That is still a question, but I think he has some ideas along those lines.

, Bill and I are still together, and I sure am glad of that. We get along swell together and we do have a lot of fun. Neither of us have any habits that are bad so there is no danger of us being led astray. The food here is good and we are both pretty healthy so there is nothing at all for you folks at home to worry about. We haven't forgotten the home folks though and you can bet your life that once we get back to the States again it will be a long time before we will ever leave and if we do it is going to take of team of mules to move us.

Bill has told me quite a bit about Dolphin Cove and I have made up my mind to come down there at least for a visit some day and then I hope to meet you. At that time, you will meet just about the sweetest, swellest, girl —my wife and I know that you will like her. She must be a lot like you, or you are a lot like her. One of the two. Anyway, I know that she is a lot of fun and enjoys sports and from what I know of you, you are a person that goes in for sports too. Bill tells me that you are lots of fun too. He had your picture here in the office for a long time and the major would really kid Bill. You should hear Bill rave about you and how you are. It is all in fun though, I mean the kidding.

Here I am stumped for words, so I guess that I had better close. I guess that you would rather hear what Bill writes than what Rick writes so I'll sign off. Take care of yourself and God bless you. I'm still your friend, I hope Rick

I just read what Rick wrote and I don't know so much about some of the things he wrote such as you had rather read what I write than his. I don't know so much about that because I can't seem to think of anything to write about. It seems that all I can do is fill up the space with a lot of nonsense. I think Rick can write a good letter when he wants to and that is something that I can't do. I can think of a thousand things to say before I start writing and then when I sit down I seem to forget what it is all about. Anyway maybe you will enjoy hearing from me, hope so anyway. Rick was speaking about the snow up on the mountain a minute ago and he says that is something that we never see in that part of the country. How about telling him about it, you know it did snow there some time ago so he can no longer say that it never has snowed in my part of the country. I have often told these birds that it gets too cold around home to snow and they don't seem to believe me. He says that is impossible it couldn't get too cold. Maybe the temperature doesn't get as low at home as it does in his part of the country, but it is a lot colder. I think, maybe it is not colder but you seem to feel it more in Dolphin Cove. You know it is almost as cold as it was hot last summer. Last summer we were in a place called "Kings Cross" the real name of the place is Souok El Khemis. I don't know if you can find it on the map, but it is there anyway. It wasn't much of a place in fact it was nothing but the field with the planes and a few miles up the road was the town shot all up of course so there wasn't anything there, just like all the rest of the places around that part of Africa. The place was so hot there that the weather station thermometer went up so high it broke and that's getting pretty hot, I've seen the weather get pretty hot around home but nothing that could compare with this over here, I have heard that this is the second hottest place in the world and I can well believe it too. Well as Rick says I am stumped for words and can't think of a thing to say so I guess I had better close for this time. I hope you excuse the typing and take all mistakes as love. How is that song "good by now." Hear it some time.

Love, "Bill"

P.S. I'll explain about the envelope. Rick addressed it and he put that "not yet" on it. What it really was is "not_____ yet". I'll explain in the next letter you'll have to overlook it this time, Love, Bill

March 4, 1944

Dearest Mary Lou,

Received two of your very sweet letters enjoyed reading them so much I just wish I could get about three or four every day but the only way I could be satisfied is to be home with you.

Someone mentioned to me in a letter I received that another guy from the gang made it home. I always like to hear about those fellows getting home, I guess this is because I can't get home myself. I know how they feel when they get home and I also know how they feel when they have to come back because I went through it all once myself. It was a wonderful feeling to be home and they will say that thing too.

I told you I sure did love your picture and I wish you would send me another one like it I would give anything to have a life-size picture of you that would be wonderful. I wish too that I could send you a picture from here. You understand how things are about that. Oh yes, and another thing in your letter you said Rick sure did tell you a lot about me and that was just what you wanted to hear. You may not know it but you and Rick have me running in circles, first I ask you what he told you, after about a week of kidding and he handed me a big line of nothing and now you say he told you a lot about me and it was just what you wanted to hear. Will you tell me what he did tell you. Maybe he let you in on a few of my secrets how do I know. And as far as his taking care of me that's simply not true. He may not be a father yet, but he sure tries to act like one and gets a lot of practice. I can't say anything to him I just let him go. You know I am a pretty big boy who has been away from his home for a pretty good time now. I think I can take care of myself by this time, I have for the last few years or so. I guess I have had too much responsibility when I was a kid to be taken over by any one now I'll tell him what you said, though, and I am sure he will take the best care of me just like a father. The new address you sent me, are you staying there while you are working or has your family, and all moved into town? How do you like living in town after living in Mossy Oak for so long? I guess it is quite a change for you. I know it was a change for me when we moved from town into Mossy Oak and after living in the community for such a long time I don't think I would like to live back in the city but that remains to be seen. I guess right now I could get used to anything because wherever I put my coat is home to me now. I don't have a home, that is why I'm in the Army anyway. I will send this letter to the address you put on the envelope with your letter, all right, until I hear different from you OK?

I think I had better explain about that envelope you received some time ago or have you. I started to the tent and asked Rick to address a letter for me and when I told him your address he saw how much alike our names are.

At the end he put "not ___ yet," and then he erased out my name. I can just about imagine what the people are going to think when some of them see that. As long as you know about it and don't mind it is OK with me I'll try and see it doesn't happen again so if you have a free moment and think of me you can drop me a line. Just that I know you are OK and in good health. That's all

Ann Cason

that matters with me. Look you take care of yourself and don't work too hard and that's an order from Sergeant Bill. Well I guess I had better close for now so for now I'll just say Goodbye for now write soon. Love Bill

March 15, 1944

Dearest Mary Lou,

Just a line tonight to say hello and that things are about the same with me. I haven't had much time in the last few days to write you so I hope you will forgive me this time.

How are things around home these days? How do you like your new home or have you moved yet? In your last letter you said you were moving on Park street. You know it has been so long since I've been around that place I can't seem to place Park street. How about a description of it in your next letter? I can't seem to remember the names of the streets or places anymore. I can get a good outline of how the city looked but that's about all. Which bus is it that's running out to the place now? Which bus was it that went through Mossy Oak? Mary Lou, it sure doesn't seem possible but the small details are things that I like to hear about and I guess all the boys like the small things of his or her own home.

The other day while coming from work one of the fellows had a camera and took a couple pictures of me and I thought you would like to see the guy you are writing to. You will have to excuse the looks because I didn't have a chance to clean up or anything, oh yes and another thing, my face wasn't really that dirty — that was a shadow across my face. If I ever get the chance to have a good picture made in my uniform I'll send you one and in the meantime how about a picture or so from you. You know I don't have but two of you, one small one and the large one you sent. Say tell me how are you and Luke making out these days? Do you hear from him often or has he been shipped overseas? You know that's a dreadful thought – to know you are going into battle. After he gets over here and sees for himself what it's like it won't be so bad. The first six months are the worst if a fellow can live through those months he can almost live through the rest of it, that of course is unless he stops a bullet.

We are going to be awarded two Bronze stars for battle participation in two major campaigns, the African and Sicilian campaigns and I suppose we will get another one soon. With all my ribbons and stars, I'm going to be all fixed up but awards are nothing, getting home is the main thing now and from what I can get from home and around my chances look pretty good. I hope they haven't been trying to mislead the public. Although I haven't heard any news of it over here, the people that I hear from say it's so, I guess there must be something to it.

Well I guess a had better close for this time, but I'll write again shortly. Take good care of yourself and I'll see you soon

Love, Bill

CHAPTER 8

Confessions

Writing to Bill was so easy. She felt as if he were in the room with her. Should she take a chance and slowly let him know her feelings for him, or should she keep the subject light and comfortable? He was asking about her personal relationship with Luke and was telling her about his relationships. Should she take a chance and open her heart to him? Could she trust him with her heart?

Mary Lou worked in the accounting department at Dolphin Cove's largest department store. It was a good job and paid well. She was well liked by her coworkers and was very proficient at her job. Sarah sat at the desk next to hers, and they would chitchat all day. They had become close friends, and sometimes the conversation would extend beyond chitchat to something deep and meaningful.

Today was one of those days.

She simply had to talk to someone about Bill and Luke. Talking with her mother was not an option; she was in "Camp Luke." Sarah knew about Luke because of the engagement ring she was wearing, but she did not know about Bill and the letters they were writing to each other.

After Mary Lou told Sarah the entire story about how her feelings for Bill had developed, she felt somewhat relieved. Sarah told her she should let Bill know how she felt. It appeared he was interested in a relationship with her and was gently trying to figure out where her heart was with Luke.

To complicate the situation, she was being pursued by an English fellow named Chris. He was quite a diversion from Bill and Luke but posed no threat for capturing her heart. Chris would take her dancing, and he asked no questions regarding the engagement ring. Their relationship was without commitment and had no future. They simply enjoyed dancing and were the best duo on the dance floor.

The walk home from work was pleasant. The slightly cool temperatures gave her a fresh energetic feeling and helped her walk at a crisp pace. She enjoyed the exercise. It helped her think, which she had a tendency to overdo. The air was filled with the fragrance of blooms from the early spring flowers, and as she walked up the steps to the front porch, the aroma from the kitchen confirmed to her the evening meal would be delicious. Her mother was a fabulous cook. Mary Lou's growing waistline could vouch for that.

After a wonderful dinner, visit with her mother, and hot bath, she retired to her bed for a much-needed peaceful night's sleep.

Mary Lou woke up to a loud clap of thunder. A strong storm covered the area with thunder, lightning, and torrential rain showers. The storm outside was nothing compared to the storm in her dream. She turned on her bedside lamp and looked at the clock. It was 2:30 in the morning. As she settled back on her pillow, she tried to make sense of the dream. She was somewhere in France and was looking for Luke and Bill. As she wandered through the unknown city, she could hear each one calling to her, and because the fog was so thick, she could not see them and did not know which way to go to find them. The bombs got louder, and their calling got louder. She began crying because she could only rescue one, and the fate of the other would never be known.

Mary Lou turned off the light and tried to sleep, but with no success. Deep in her soul was a battle unlike any ever fought. How did one solve the issues of the heart without anyone getting hurt? When you loved two people in two different ways, which one did you choose? She resolved for the night to let those questions rest. Maybe she would also.

April 5, 1944

Dearest Mary Lou,

Received your very sweet letters a couple of days ago, but just haven't had time to write. Speaking of mail, I haven't had a letter from you in a long time.

Ann Cason

But I guess they have been keeping you quite busy at home. Just write when you can and have time, so you won't forget me.

That must have been quite a dream you had when you wrote the letter. It could have been a little better though if I had really been there. You will probably think you are dreaming when I do come home because the first thing you know I'm going to walk in the store and then you will be surprised. That's the way I did the folks the last time I came home. I didn't let anyone know I was coming. That way it seems to be more fun than if they were expecting me. If they had been expecting me they would have half killed themselves trying to fix for me. That's alright for some other people but I'm just a simple sort of fellow. To see you right now would be almost like marrying a queen, I'll tell you it would be almost too good to be true. Someday I hope I'll get the chance to see you again.

I haven't had any mail from the fellows in fact I haven't had any mail much at all. I wrote to Flora's husband last night, she sent me his address so I thought I would drop him a line.

Mary Lou what ever became of your English boyfriend? Is he still around? In one of your letters some time ago you asked me what I thought about him. If you like the guy and he is ok well date him but for myself if I can't show the American girls a good time I won't date any over here. The first thing is there is none over here and if they were I wouldn't date them. As I said before, I'll take my chances back in the States. Don't know what my chances will be but never-the-less there is nothing like hometown girls. I have you to come home to don't I?

Well I guess I had getter close for this time, but I'll write again. Take care of yourself and I hope to see you very soon. Write soon.

Love, Bill

Mary Lou could tell when Bill had been on a mission. His letters were short and light in content. She knew he was in combat, but he never talked about the details. Maybe it was because of the restrictions and how their letters would be censored, or maybe it was because the whole concept of war was too painful to repeat. None of the letters from Bill or Rick discussed the details of where they were or what they were doing. But at least they were writing. It meant they were alive. The thought of Luke or Bill "taking a bullet," as they would say, was more than she could comprehend. She prayed every time she opened a letter it would say in the opening paragraph, "Just wanted you to know I am well and okay." It was difficult for her to comprehend the conditions the soldiers were forced to endure, when she had a nice, warm bed with clean sheets and food on the table.

While Bill and Mary Lou fought the war within themselves, a war to end all wars was being fought by innocent young men and women who were at the mercy of high-ranking government officials making life and death decisions. Destruction was taking place in all four corners of the world.

On April 4, 1944, the first stage of the Battle of Imphal ended. The Japanese failed to destroy the Allied defense line. The British Fourth Corps now could turn its attention to the destruction of the Japanese.[4]

On April 15, 1944, it was decided by the US Eighth Army Air Force and the RAF Bomber Command to change the bombing of German urban centers to railroads in Belgium and France. This was in preparation for the upcoming Allied invasion. This change would prevent German reinforcements from reaching the front line. The effort of 448 Flying Fortresses and Liberators of the US Fifteenth Army Air Force that were escorted by 150 Mustang fighters proved to be a successful attack on the oil fields at Ploesti in the Romanian capital, Bucharest.[5]

On April 22, 1944, in the Pacific, General Douglas MacArthur established a new base for Operation Cartwheel in Hollandia, in northern New Guinea, by making an amphibious landing with Allied forces of 52,000 strong. Operation Cartwheel was designed to drive the Japanese from northwest New Guinea.[6]

One mission from North Africa to the mainland of Italy, a key transportation center near Naples, was the target of thirty-six aircraft of the 310th Bomb Group. Enemy fighters tried unsuccessfully to divert the B-25 formation. The mission was successful in destroying the railroad marshalling yards and eighteen of the attacking fighters, but it came at a high price. The 310th Group lost three aircraft, and the remaining ships that returned were filled with flak and bullet holes. This mission earned one of the two Distinguished Unit citations for the 310th.[7]

How did they do it? How did they keep their sanity? How did they make it day after day? *The letters,* she thought. *They always ask for letters.* She promised herself she would do all she could do to continue to write letters to those guys who sacrificed so much for her.

CHAPTER 9
Ellie

April 24, 1944

Dearest Mary Lou,

Received your most welcomed letter and sure was glad to hear from you. From your letter everything must be still ok back home. You are still working pretty hard I bet, well don't try to take on too much of a job and run your health down, that isn't good.

I'm sorry Mary Lou that I haven't written in such a long time but things with me have been pretty busy. I haven't had time to write home and I know the folks are worried about me. I hope you will forgive me this time and I'll try not to let it happen again. Also, I hope you will excuse the letter because I'm awful tired and don't feel much like writing but if I don't write some now I want have a chance again for a while, I'll try to make the best of this chance.

From the way you talk the place where you are living is a beautiful place. I didn't tell you, but Dad bought another place a few months ago. And he says it's also very pretty. I hope one day shortly I can see some of those places that you and the folks at home have been telling me about. I bet it's beautiful around Dolphin Cove now with spring here and everything I wish I was back to enjoy some of it, to look at the bright blossom of the dogwood and see all the flowers—I bet it's sure pretty. It does make it a little better for your work doesn't it – I mean to be living in town.

I haven't had a letter from any of the old gang out in Mossy Oak with the exception of Flora. I had a couple letters from her. She says her health is good, but she isn't feeling so hot. She told me she was expecting the stork sometime in July that isn't so long off, is it? Well I hope she pulls through ok; I know she will be proud and a very good mother to her son or daughter. If Franklin was there with her I know she would feel a lot better but like she said they all have to go sometimes, and it was just his time to be transferred. As far as the rest of the gang is concerned I don't know much about them.

I have something funny to tell you. Rick said that you would be married in four months. He said he just knew it because he had a feeling that you would be. How about that, is it so? By the way how is the situation in Dolphin Cove for dates? I don't guess there is too many men left around there is it. Well as I said before Mary Lou, I'm just about dead on my feet so I think I had better close. Be sweet and write soon

Love Bill

April 30, 1944

Dearest Mary Lou,

Received two of your very sweet letters and sure was glad to hear from you. You know it had been a good little while but since you said you had company I think I understand. I know you and I will have a wonderful time when I get home so I'm looking forward to that day.

Yes, Mary Lou, in my last letter I guess I was a little blue and I don't think I should have written that because when I feel like that I usually say things that I don't want to say. Things back home don't worry me, but it does seem strange that I never noticed the things that I had when I was home. It took the Army and the war to make me see things clearly. I'm afraid if I had stayed in Dolphin Cove I would have messed up a couple nice peoples' lives and I didn't want to do that so the best thing to do was to leave. I realized now some of the mistakes I made but it still hasn't changed my feelings toward Flora. I know, I said I didn't care anymore about her and all that but I still feel the same about her as I did the day I left and I guess I will continue to feel that way until I get home and can get around enough people to forget her. She is married now and is having a baby so I'm not even in her mind but that still doesn't keep me from loving her, why I don't know because I know she loves her husband and I know he loves her. Hey you know I kind of think I'm talking to much about one subject I don't like to think about. You said if I worry too much I want be any good when I get home. I don't worry about anything enough to run down my health in fact I don't even worry about myself that much. I've just about come to the conclusion that if anything is going to happen there isn't anything I or anyone else can do to stop it. If I get it in a plane crash or anything else it will just be my time but you can believe me I'm not going to have that day come along if I can help it but of course that's something I will not know anything about, but oh well why talk about that.

You know I can't think of anything to write about. I can't talk about what happens here and I don't know what is going on at home so there just isn't much I can really talk about. I have had a good life in the Army though that was back in the states. I met a guy when I first came in the Army, his name is Troy and this guy James lived next door to us at home so the three of us were even closer than brothers. We use to go down to his home and spend the weekend about every week. He has two sisters which were very nice to me. I went with one of them as long as I was in the states. She even came to South Carolina. where the three of us were. Yes, we use to have quite a time while in the States. Well I guess I had better close for this time but I'll write again in a day or so. Be sweet and write soon. Love Bill.

Ann Cason

May 4, 1944

Dearest Mary Lou,

Just a line to say I'm still ok and never felt better in my life. In the first letter I'm afraid I wasn't quite up to par. I guess I wasn't feeling any too good, just one of those things you know we all have our ups and downs.

In one of the letters you wrote you were speaking about Easter. What happened around home? I bet it was a pretty Easter this year, I sure will be glad to see the pictures you all made, I wish I could send you some more but I have not been able to make any. I have a few shots I would like for you to see but they won't let me send them through the mail. They say it is bad for the morale of the civilian population. I'll show you all the pictures I have made when I get home. Mary Lou do you think I have changed as much as you say? You know, I think everyone changes to suit the surroundings so therefore in a matter of speaking, I guess I have changed some and another thing, I'm not going to give up no matter what happens, I guess I've got too much waiting for me at home and back in the States for anything like that. don't worry about me quitting. I'm still going just as strong as the day we came into Casablanca. I'm still young yet and I've got a long life ahead of me. That life is going to depend on myself and I'm going to make it a happy one because we only live once. I can't say much about the life I'm living here because it isn't very pleasant but I'm holding on until I can really start living. Just think when all the fellows come home and get out of the Army and start life all over again. It's going to take me longer to get use to civilian life again than it took for the Army, but do I worry, no way, I'm sitting on top of the world.

Well you know it's getting close to chow time and if I don't get this letter mailed it will be that much longer getting there. Better close. Be sweet and I'll see you very soon

Love, Bill

Mary Lou tried to see the clear picture, with no success. Luke loved Mary Lou, Mary Lou loved Bill, Bill loved Flora, and Flora was married to Franklin and having a baby. What a tangled web of emotion. Fighting a war on top of all that was enough to cause anyone to snap. But somehow Mary Lou kept going and kept writing. Something had to break, and soon!

Mary Lou was in desperate need of a vacation from the struggles of war. She and Sarah took a road trip to New Orleans, where they rested and enjoyed the nightlife.

While Mary Lou took a breather from her struggles, the Allies launched the greatest amphibious operation in history. The statistics for the invasion force were staggering: 50,000 men for the initial assault; more than 2 million men to be shipped to France in all, comprising a total thirty-nine divisions; 139 major warships, with 221 smaller combat vessels; more than 1,000 minesweepers and auxiliary vessels; 4,000 landing craft; 805 merchant ships; fifty-nine blockships; three hundred miscellaneous small craft; and 1,000 aircraft, including fighters, bombers, transports, and gliders. In addition, the invasion force had the support of more than 100,000 members of the French resistance, who launched hit-and-run attacks on German targets.[8]

D-Day, the Allied invasion of Normandy, code-named Operation Overlord, began with the assault of three airborne divisions—the US Eighty-Second and 101st on the right flank of the US forces and the British Sixth Airborne on the left flank of the British—while seaborne forces landed on five beaches. The Germans made their one major counterattack between Juno and Sword but were defeated.

By day's end, the Allies had a toehold in German-occupied Europe, at a cost of 2,500 lives.[9]

CHAPTER 10

Reenactment

May 19, 1944

Dearest Mary Lou,

Received your very sweet letter and sure was glad to hear from you. You know it has been quite some time now since I've heard from you but I guess I haven't been writing too much either. I'll tell you the truth I just haven't had time to write any one much.

I knew you had not forgotten me just because you did not write. I understand how things are and I guess you are working pretty long so when you don't write for a while I know you can't write. Just a line once in a while to say hello and that you have not forgotten me and to let me know you are ok. Say speaking about coming home, from the way it looks over here it want be long now and I'm going to hold you to that promise you made for showing me a good time. I know it may sound funny to you but I'm going to need someone to teach me how to go about things again, I've just about forgot all I knew about the ways of civilian life but once I get back I don't think it will take me long to catch on again.

Leaving home wasn't so bad because I left on my own. But in a way it wasn't so good either. I left all the old things I once knew, all my old friends for an entirely new life. I counted on the new life for a good change and to more or less get acquainted with the world. But I didn't exactly want this kind of life. I guess I have learned just about all I care to about the foreign countries of the world and now I want to get back and see how our own country lives. In the very near future, I expect to do quite a lot of traveling when I return to the States and get out of the Army.

Sure wish I could be home with you when you get your vacation. Wouldn't we take in the town? I'll tell you what, I will not be there when you have your nine day vacation in June but I'll be with you when you get your two weeks next year. That is a long way off to be making a date isn't it, but what can we do that's the only thing there is left to do. You asked me would I like it if you took another vacation when I get home to be with me. You bet I would like it, in fact I couldn't think of anything better. It's almost too good to think about, a two weeks furlough, plenty of money and you to show me the ropes again, what a deal that would be.

I bet the pictures sure are good of you and I'm looking forward to seeing them. You said in a few letters ago that you would send me some but I guess you just forgot about it. I think it is just about as hard to get pictures in the States as it is over here isn't it? Collecting pictures and making them is my hobby so anything you have, any pictures you don't want send them on over. I would love to see all you in person but until such time I can get home I'll just settle for a few pictures of you.

Well guess I had better close for this time but I'll write again soon. Oh yes, Rick said tell you hello.

P.S. Tell Flora I said hello, will you, just plain Bill

Love Bill

While in New Orleans, Mary Lou and Sarah attended a reenactment of the landing on the beaches of Normandy hosted by Higgins Industries, who supplied the amphibious boats for the troops. It was a celebration of the 10,000[th] boat delivered to the US Navy. The reenactment took place on the shore of Lake Pontchartrain in New Orleans. It was an impressive display of power and strength of the ground forces of the US Army and Navy.[10]

As Mary Lou and Sarah watched the reenactment of D-Day, military aircraft, including B-26 and B-29 bombers, flew overhead. They learned the planes were being piloted by women. Mary Lou knew she needed to investigate this amazing sight.

With the onset of war, the United States was experiencing a shortage of pilots. It was suggested to the leadership that they train women to fly military aircraft so male pilots could fly combat missions overseas. The first graduating class of Women Air Force Service Pilots (WASP) was in 1944. US Army Commanding General Henry "Hap" Arnold said he wasn't sure whether a slip of a girl could fight the controls of a B-17 in heavy weather. General Arnold also said, as the ceremony was closing, "In 1944, it is on the record women can fly as good as men."

These women ferried planes such as the B-26 and the B-29 bombers from factories to military bases and places throughout the US mainland. They tested overhauled planes and towed targets so ground and air gunners could perform training maneuvers *with live ammunition*. The United States trained male pilots from scratch. But the WASP came into the program with a knowledge of flying. The head of the WASP program was Jacqueline Cochran, a pioneer aviator whose job it was to train thousands of women to fly for the army. In the process, she discovered the women's safety records were comparable to or better than their male counterparts.[11]

It was difficult for the loved ones of those fighting the war to comprehend the horrific scenes of destruction and death, and the soldiers were not allowed to talk about it. Letters to home consisted mostly of small talk and the status of the soldier's health and well-being. The event by Higgins Industries changed the way Mary Lou thought about the war and the men who were giving their all to preserve her freedoms. Her "vacation" took on a new meaning. A little embarrassed by her selfishness, she and Sarah decided to cut their vacation short and return home.

June 26, 1944

Dearest Mary Lou,

Just a few lines to say I received your letter and sure was glad to hear from you. I sorry I did not answer your letter sooner but to tell you the truth I just haven't had time, you know how things are. I do not have much time right now to write but I'm going to take a few minutes to answer your letter before I'm not able to answer it.

I'm glad you had a chance for a vacation. I know it sure did you good to get away for a while. From the way you write about it you must have had quite a time. I'm glad for you because you are such a sweet girl. Every time you have a chance to go someplace, have a good time and above all don't let this war worry you. It is going to be over soon and I'll be home to take you for a good time. Say you know I never thought about it but where shall we go, do you have any idea of a place in or around Dolphin Cove. I got a paper and it said most of the places were off limits to servicemen. Oh well we'll worry about that when I return home, ok?

Mary Lou, nothing worries me anymore. I just take like as it comes, if it is rough that's too bad for me but if it's a good nice clean life that is my good luck. I don't worry about any of them I'll take the bad with the good.

I understand how it was for you. You must think a lot of me to write when you are so tired. Thanks a lot Mary Lou, you are one girl in a million.

Guess I'd better close for this time. Maybe I'll have more time pretty soon. Write soon.

Lots of love, Bill

Her heart was about to burst with joy. He was making plans for his future, and she was in it! Mary Lou finally took Sarah's advice and began to share her feelings with Bill. She was testing the waters to see if he was really serious about a relationship with her. She put it plainly to him about his relationship with Flora. He had to accept the fact she was married to Franklin and was building a life and family with him. Mary Lou was anxiously waiting for a response from him, but she never expected what he wrote.

Bill waited a while before addressing the topic of Mary Lou's feelings for him. It was a delicate situation, and he wanted to handle it in the right way. Yes, he was romantically interested in her, but she was officially engaged to another man. He simply could not be the cause of the dissolution of that relationship. Losing Flora was bad enough on him emotionally and adding home-wrecker to his résumé was not exactly what he wanted. He had preserved his moral state with the gang when he gracefully left for the army air corps after Flora married Franklin. He was not sure, however, he would receive the same support from the members of the gang if he was the cause of the breakup of the gang's most liked couple.

CHAPTER 11

People, Plans, Promises

July 1, 1944

Dear Mary Lou,

Received your very sweet letter and sure was glad to hear from you. I see by your letter that most everything around home is still the same and I'm glad to hear it.

I bet you sure had a swell time on your vacation. Just wait until I come home and then I'll show you a really nice time. It sure has been a long time since I have been on a date with a girl that I'm almost afraid to try it. I think you could take me in tow and show me the ropes again, it will take but one date with you and then I'll be my old self again.

Rick said he was surprised you were not married. He said it seemed that everyone there was getting married and that you were such a popular girl with the boys he didn't see how you could get around it. Well marriage in my opinion is something you can't jump into right in the moment or you'll be sorry. A few of the girls around the place have but how they are making out I wouldn't know. I hope to be married one of these days and from the way it looks I'll have to find one over here before I'm too old. You said if you were to come over here could you find someone to marry. Let me tell you something, *if you came over here looking for a husband it would take you about three seconds to find one. I know you look beautiful in your evening dress but it sure didn't take an evening dress to make you beautiful, I sure will be glad when the pictures get here. I don't think I told you but I can't send any more from here. They won't let us. You will have to save them for me when I come home so I can see you. You asked me how I would like that, all I can say is "I'd love it." It does not matter to me what kind of clothes you are wearing, just being with you would be heaven. You are beautiful from the inside to the outside. You bet we'll go any place you would like to go. Okay, we'll take in the whole town together. I tell you you're going to lose a lot of sleep because it's going to take me a long time to catch up and you can count on me being at your place to pick you up every night. We'll take in the beach and have a wonderful time together. By-the-way can you dance? You're going to teach me how again because I don't think I can anymore. I wish I could have been there when you made the ice cream. How my mouth watered when I read that. I sure would like for you to send me some but I'm afraid that's impossible. Don't worry we will have plenty when I get home. My favorite kind is walnut, I love it but have not seen any for years. Well I guess I had better close, got a tough day ahead of me tomorrow. Write soon I hope to be home soon,*

Love, Bill

The month of July was a busy time for those assigned to the 310th Bomb Group. Eighteen combat missions were flown along with four nickeling missions. Along with a full schedule of combat missions, the 310th Bomb Group participated in a general inspection by the inspector general and his staff of fifteen officers. It was a happy reunion on July 2, 1944, when one of their own pilots, who was reported a prisoner of war by the Italian government on April 14, 1943, was returned to the 310th group. Military regulations required all experiences during his capture and the details of his escape to be classified as top secret. They were just glad he was returned. After some rest and debriefing, he was returned to the United States.

The month of July 1944 also brought a long-awaited event: the championship softball tournament between the 381st group and the 340th group. The 381st won the tournament 4–0 and then traveled to Ajaccio on July 29, 1944, to play the 976th Signal Company for the title championship of southern Corsica. The 381st returned on July 30, 1944, with the championship title after winning the second game with a score of 3–2.[12]

July 11, 1944

Dearest Mary Lou,

Received your very sweet letter and sure was glad to hear from you. I hope you can understand why I haven't been writing much lately. They have had me pretty busy I will put it down to that.

How are things going on the old home front, just as I thought. With you on the job what could go wrong. By the way, I bet you all are having quite a time of it now that it's getting so hot but I know you are at the beach lot. I would like to be there with you right now with the full moon and just to hear the ocean and the music from the dance hall. With you there with me I couldn't ask for anything better. You know it is this kind of an evening that I think about home most. Right now everything is quiet for a change, it's so peaceful and I can't help but think about the good times we could be having back at home. If I were only home right now you and I would probably be swimming in the moonlight. Can you swim? If you can't I am a very good teacher. I taught a girl to swim, she liked to have drown me. I am sure you wouldn't because I would never let go of you long enough. I know this peacefulness can't last for long something is bound to turn up. Come to think about it I never did receive the picture you were going to send me, how about enclosing a picture postcard of good old Dolphin Cove so I can see what the place looks like. Any kind just any kind will do, I'd appreciate pictures of any kind just send them.

Well it's getting a little late now and I must close, but I'll remember that date. You can start planning now and meanwhile I'll dream about you tonight ok? You don't mind appearing in my dreams, do you? Good night dear, Love Bill

July 27, 1944

Dearest Mary Lou,

Received your sweet letter and was glad to hear from you. It's been a pretty good while since I had any mail from anyone and the first letter I get right after this long time is from you. I think that's pretty wonderful. Thanks very much for the picture. You know you almost startled me, I never realized you were so beautiful. I haven't seen you in so long I didn't realize just what I am missing. Are we going to make up for lost time when I get home, I think the evening gown you have on is very lovely, I think it was made especially for you because no one else could be as lovely as you are. When you send things like that it sure does build up my morale. When I see pictures of what I'm coming home to it makes me go that much harder. It looks as if I might have a little trouble when take you out because of all the fellows will want to cut in on me. Remember when I get home the first date is with you and none of this cutting in business. I'm pretty much of a hog, am I not. You bet we'll have a good time but of course you will have to take me by the hand and sort of teach me the ropes and show me around. You see, I've been away from Dolphin Cove so long I've forgotten all those places. That's something I won't worry about, while I'm with you I will not worry about anything. You know Dolphin Cove and you know the best places so I'll leave it entirely up to you. Anything you like I'll love it.

On 4 July all I did was mark off another day. There was plenty of fireworks that day but no one was celebrating. It was a very beautiful day and sort of made me wish I was home. I was sure every one of those had a good time but if you say it rained I don't guess there was much going on. You know you can't have a picnic in the rain. I don't care if it is raining when I get home we are going to spend the day at the beach or something, rain or no rain. Are you willing? There is no such thing as celebrating a holiday over here that is with the exception of Christmas that's about the only one. One day is just like the next. I'm going to wait and do my celebrating with you when I get back to the States that would really be something to celebrate.

Has Flora had her baby yet? She wrote and said it was to be born in July. I answered her letter but haven't received another letter from her. Oh well, I guess she doesn't feel much like writing. Just wait until I come home and I'll take you out to Mossy Oak and that's not the only place we'll go either, we'll take in all of Dolphin Cove.

I had better close for this time but I'll write again as I can. Take care yourself and write soon I'll see you soon.

Love Bill

July 31, 1944

Dear Mary Lou,

Received your very sweet letter and sure enjoyed hearing from you for the past 15 or 20 days I have not had any mail but the last couple of days are coming through wonderful. Your letter was dated July 20 so you can see it didn't take it too long to come over. I hope the letters I have been writing you get there as quick as yours come here. That will be like the mail in the States don't you think.

Ann Cason

From the way you say you are not married yet you sound as if you expect to be pretty soon. Do you have a steady boyfriend you are in love with or something? I guess all the good fellows are in the service. I think you had better wait until the boys get back home I know you will be married when they come, because I can't see how a beautiful girl like you could stay single. I can't see how you have stayed single this far, I bet lots of guys have asked you to be their wife? How about it, have they? I have never thought about marrying but once and I think you can imagine who that was but oh well I guess she didn't love me. She was married all right but not to me I haven't thought much about it. I could have been married a dozen times but it never appealed to me since Flora left me. I guess I'll get married one of these days but since Flora and I broke up I haven't seen enough of any girl to know enough about them to marry. I'll have plenty of time when I returned to the States don't you think? Say there is something I'd like to ask you. Did she ever mention anything about me? I'd really like to know about how she feels about me now that she is married you don't have to mention to her anything I've said concerning this. You know I truly believe she was in love with me once I don't have to tell you how much I was in love with her but it's all over now and I'll do my best to forget her. I can't get her off my mind now but I know the first time I take you out I can guarantee I won't have her on my mind it will be strictly you and no one but you. You can make anyone forget their troubles especially me. I love that soft little gleam in your eyes. You know in the picture you sent me you look as if you are ready to speak to me. You look so beautiful so natural it looks as though I could walk right up and take you in my arms without any trouble at all and you believe me I would if I could. Thanks a million Mary Lou for the postcards and pictures of yourself you are sending I know I'll love them.

You don't have to worry about making me forget what I've been through with once I'm with you. I'm sure I won't be thinking about the past because my mind will be entirely on you and the future good times we will have.

I told Rick what you said about being married and he said he would give you a little more time. Just wait. I'm saying you had better not be married when I get home. It will save a lot of trouble and remember you have a date with me. I don't think you will be married I am depending on you too much. A little about the mail situation now. I have used every minute of my spare time to write you these last few days but when the time comes that I won't have the chance to write don't think I don't want to write because I really do. I think you understand so let's forget about that. Now a little about the "male" situation. My health is still fine and I'm feeling pretty good the only thing wrong with me is that I want to come home. Guess I'd better close. Write soon,

Love, Bill

It was business as usual for the 310th during the month of August 1944. Twenty-five combat missions and two nickeling missions were flown against enemy lines in Northern Italy for a total of 241 sorties. One aircraft was lost in action, but its crew returned safely to the base. On August 2, 1944, a formal presentation of awards to the combat men of the squadron was officiated by Brigadier General Knapp. During this presentation, roll was called, and more than a few officers and enlisted men were absent. The absentees were required to drill for one hour each evening until further notice.

August 15, 1944, began with a briefing at 4:00 a.m., at which time details of the day's mission were discussed. The mission would directly support the ground forces that were to invade southern France at 7:30 a.m. Before the crews reached their planes, the entire base was aware of the day's mission. It was an anxious day as the squadron awaited the return of the planes. At noon, the BBC reported a beachhead had been established and there were few casualties. Three missions were flown to southern France, and it was a very busy and successful day for the 310th Group.[13]

CHAPTER 12

A Changed Man

August 8, 1944

Dearest Mary Lou

Well now that I have a little time I just think I'll sit down and drop the couple lines. Don't mind do you? Things are pretty quiet about now and I want something to keep my mind off the war and among other things I wanted to write to you. I just got back from chow a minute ago but wasn't any too good, it was spam and if I ever see another piece of spam as long as I live that will be too soon. I sure hate the stuff. That is about all we have for one whole winter and I've never been so tired of any one thing in my life. But let's get down to something a little more pleasant. What you say we talk about you for a while. How have you been since the last time I wrote you just fine I hope, been doing a lot of swimming lately, bet you have and I know I sure couldn't blame you because if the heat is as bad there as it is here I think I'd stay in the water all the time. That Dolphin Cove Beach would sure come in handy about now too. Right now it's about 8:30 PM and you would think it would be a little cool but to tell you the truth it is just as hot right now as it was at 12 o'clock if not a little hotter I 'm sure there sure are plenty of people over at the beach nowadays and as bad as I hate a crowds I think I could stand a little of it. There is plenty of beach so I don't think I would have to worry about finding a place that wasn't so crowded, I could always walk down the beach and go swimming

Tell me, how is your work been coming along these days, are you still working at the store? They keep you pretty busy don't they, but don't let it get you down the war can't last forever and then I think you're probably getting married and won't have to work then. The only thing you have to keep house for your husband if you would call that work. I know some women do but to tell you the truth I wouldn't' know about those things because I have never kept house. I can't see how you have gone this long without being married I know all the rest of the girls around the place are either married or engaged. What are you waiting on, do you have a boyfriend over here that you are waiting for?. I know marriage is a serious thing you can't just marry anyone, you need to have the right one before doing anything like that. When I do get married it will be someone that I love not just a girl that I think a lot of and she is going to be in love with me too. Like in one case I was involved in before, I love the girl but she didn't love me if we had been married we probably wouldn't have made a go of it because someone else was in her mind. In a way I'm glad that I didn't get married, just look at the length of time that I have been over here and think that if I had a wife how long she would have to wait for me. I guess she would always be worried about me and I would be the same about her. The only contact we would have would be through the mail and that is no way to build on a marriage. How did I get on that subject? I can get started on some of the craziest things. I just let my thoughts run and you see the results that come out, not very clear are they? Nothing is clear to me any more I think I live in a daze now days. The time I want to wake up is when they sound the bell for a landing in the harbor in the United States. When I get back I'm going to be a one-man invasion force on Dolphin Cove. That's my objective and I know before long I'll gained that objective. I know the going is going to be tough, but I'll have to have someone to lead me through the dark spots do you think you can handle that assignment? I think I need someone to show me the town again because I think I've just about forgot the place and I know the place has changed. since I've been away. So you see unless I have somebody to show me this high spots I will miss them. That's just like going into a town that you don't know but if you can find someone that knows the place and can take you around you have a lot better time, see what I mean?

Have you heard from any of the other fellows lately? What happened to Luke, is he still writing you? Ah yes, there is something else I wanted to ask you I see in the Dolphin Cove paper there is a picture of a serviceman who they say is going to preflight training in California. Do you know who that is? I saw the picture that they put in the paper, but the article explaining who it was, was not legible due to some postal damage. I think I know who it is but I'm not sure. I sure would like to find out about the all of the fellows in the old community.

Well I haven't received much mail from the folks at home in the last few days, but I guess all the people around there it's pretty busy aren't they. Maybe they will write when they have a chance. Say your mail has been coming in pretty good lately and I'm sure glad to see it too because it had been sometime since I heard from you I'm sorry that I don't have any more time to write but I think you understand that don't you. Things go pretty fast over here once they get started and then there is no turning back. I'm carrying your picture in my wallet so I can see you all the time. Every time I look at the picture of you get more beautiful. I really like that evening dress you have on. When I was in Rome, I saw one just like it the one you had on and I thought about you. I looked at the price on the dress they had there and they wanted $100 for it and you know I came within an inch of buying it. Don't know what kept me from it unless it was the thought of getting it home.

What have you to hear from Flora lately? How is she getting along now that she has a son. I bet that she sure is proud of him isn't she. Say tell me what did she name him? When you see her tell her I said hello will you. I had

Dearest Mary Lou

a letter from Miss Leonard the other day and she told me about it. She said Flora was doing fine that's how I know the baby was a boy she told me.

Mary Lou there is nothing that happened over here that the government will let me tell you about that there is no news from the world of war from this correspondence. I can tell you that my health is still fine and I'm okay. I think I'm in a little better spirit today that I have been in for some time. Why I don't know unless it's the thought of the war, it sure looks good and from the way it's going we are going to keep that date before you know it. One of these days I'm going to walk in on you. I want to get a little information on you. What time of the day can I catch you at home and what time do you work You see if I get there at 2 o'clock I don't want to have to go out to your house if you are in town. What time of day can I find you at home and what times do you work? What nights are usually free you know I wouldn't want to cut in on someone else. What in the world am I talking about? From the way I talk it looks as if I'm going to come home now doesn't it. But don't pay any attention to me I'm just talking through my hat.

Well you know I think I had better close and get a little sleep, I'm sure going to need it tomorrow but I'll write again pretty soon in the meantime take care of yourself and write when you get a chance I hope you can send more pictures soon.

Love Bill

August 31, 1944

Dearest Mary Lou

Received two of your very sweet letters last night and sure was glad to hear from you. Thanks a million for the postcards, they sure are nice to see. I see if Dolphin Cove looks that way when I return, I won't have any trouble getting back into the old groove.

I'm sorry about that last letter you know the one that I sounded so blue in. I seems to have myself in trouble about the way I was feeling at the time because I wrote most everyone. Well I'll tell you between your letter and the one I received from my other girl you two have straighten me out about a few things. I never really saw myself until I received the letters and since then I can see just a kind of a fool I have been and since then my feelings toward her have completely changed. I'm not kidding either I can't see why I couldn't think of some of the things myself maybe I did but I didn't believe it until you told me. Everything is fine now and I'm a changed man. When I write about Flora now it's not the same. I don't know what was wrong with me but at any rate everything is okay now I think you have the right idea about not going with any one boy because you say it will get you in trouble I didn't think it was okay once but now I just can't see it. I don't know why I did then, but those days are past now. It is the best idea to wait until after the war is over to get married, that way you and your husband will not be away from each other. In times like these a person can't very well tell what's going to happen or where he's going to be. It may be after the war is over before I'll get married myself. Say tell me who is the guy that is so far away you will have to wait for? Send me his address, I'd like to write him a couple lines. I bet I can just about guess who it is right now, but I don't know his address is it Luke? That's it isn't it? Well Mary Lou I guess I had better try to get some sleep this time, but I'll write again as soon as I can "night."

Love Bill

As the September weather continued to dominate the activities for the 310th, combat missions were at a high level, with nineteen missions and 232 sorties flown. Although many of the communications targets in Northern Italy were heavily defended by antiaircraft guns, there were no losses of aircraft or crew. The social life of the members of the squadron increased dramatically when the officers club arranged for Saturday night dances at the enlisted men's club. The communications section of the squadron held the title of champions of the baseball tournament and made way for the football teams to entertain the troops. Life was not all about war!

September 3, 1944

Dear Mary Lou,

Received your letter and sure was glad to hear from you your letter brings very much encouragement to me while being so far from civilization.

There is something that I want to explain, and I don't quite know how. It's about a little something that you mentioned in your letter. When I said that I was glad you were waiting for me I didn't quite mean it the way that you took it, I meant that I was glad that you were keeping me a place saved for a date and that's what I want you to do too, there is really nothing between you and I but a good old-fashioned friendship that I wouldn't do anything in the world to break up. In a way of speaking you are my girl, pal, friend and anything else you might think of to complete a good friendship. You have been so good to me by writing since I've been over here, I don't think I could ever repay you.

As far as the reason for my letters mushy as a way of putting it that's all in fun. I try to talk to you in the letter just like I would to my best pal. You know sort of make a few comments and then a little kidding on the side for laughs. That's the way I like to receive letters from you. Letters mean so much to the fellows here and when I get one from a pal like you it's more fun than anything. I really do get so much enjoyment from your letters and that is the reason I want you to wait and give me a chance for a date. It seems as if that is about the only way, I'm going to repay you. I want to take you and show you the best time in your life.

I know you have someone that you are waiting for and I also have a sweet girl waiting for me. The sweetest girl waiting for me in the world. She took Flora's place years ago, but you see Flora did mean a lot to me once and right now she is a good Pal or might I say friend and I'm kinda interested in her welfare. That's one reason I ask about her so much. There is one thing I will give you and Ellie credit for and that is opening my eyes to myself. Oh yes Ellie is the girl I mentioned, I must introduce you two sometime. I'm going to Georgia when I get home and I'm thinking pretty strongly of bringing her home with me, no not to get married just to meet the folks etc.

Mary Lou keep writing just like you have it's nice to get letters from you and please don't change, just take me and my letters as one of your best pals, that is the way I want it to be. When you feel like writing and correcting me about something or tell me what you think of me how dumb I am or anything you might want to say just write it, I love it because it's so much fun. That sort of gives me an opening to make a funny remark to you and make it a game. Mary Lou, I hope you see what I'm talking about I wouldn't do anything in the world to break you and Luke up if that's who it is. I don't try to write a serious letter, but you know sometimes under certain conditions I can't help it, I know you understand that part., I don't want you to take me the wrong way. When I say something like I'm in love with you, you could tell me no one but a mother could love a face like that. Anything you want to write or anything you think about write it down don't be afraid you will hurt my feelings because you can't. If the fellows did not tease one another over here all the time sometimes I think, I would go crazy. You remember Rick, well he's a good one for that. You should hear what he thinks of me and he is another one that tells me to my face like a brother, I just told him what I said, and he said he would drop you a line. But everything is fine with me and things over here look better every day. Mary, I hope you understand what I have been gabbing about I guess I had better sleep for now, write every chance you get. I'll write and tell you the news later.

PS thanks for the post cards.

Love Bill

Dearest Mary Lou

September 2, 1944

Hello Mary Lou,

Long time no see, long time no write. I guess that I've been neglecting but I haven't been meaning to. You know how it is, there is a war going on and that keeps us busy. Things with us haven't changed since I wrote you last time and I still have to put up with this tent mate, the Dolphin Cove Playboy, and he gets worse all the time. My brother is stationed down there in Dolphin Cove and I hope he doesn't get like Bill is. I hope you take the things he says to you with a grain of salt. He will say one thing and then mean another and I pity anyone that might believe him and get their hopes up or down because he's only kidding. He sure is a lot of fun and full of surprises too. We get along well and I know that you, are one of his truest friends. He told me that he thinks of you as one of the family that you kid him along and that you have a lot of fun with your writing back and forth. That's what we sure need over here. Keep up the good work. You and he will have some good laughs one of these days when you and your husband meet him and his wife. You can talk over the old letters and make your spouse's jealous. Well it is almost midnight so I'm going to bed and I'll slip this letter into Bill's when I mail it and he won't know it. Hope I meet you soon and keep writing, Rick

Mary Lou was not prepared for this. Her heart was destroyed. How in the world could she have been so blind? She knew he was writing to Ellie, but she did not know what he was saying to her. His letters were getting more and more personal with more and more plans for the future with her. She was drawn into them and was in love with him. She was so wounded by this she could not eat or sleep. She was at risk of losing her job, and Sarah was very concerned about her.

Her mother figured it out and knew her daughter was suffering from a broken heart. It was time for her to step in and help put her daughter back together. Although she was from "Camp Luke," she also knew the heart of a woman needed passion and romance. She patiently explained to her daughter love was fickle but life was forever, and the decisions we made had consequences. We had to be prepared to bear them, good or bad. She explained that Bill was in a very fragile condition. Death and total destruction were all around him, and he was responsible for some of it personally, for pulling the trigger on an innocent life bound by commitment of government officials. To pull away from him now, seeking to protect her own broken heart, would be like pulling the trigger on Bill. She must pull herself together, face reality, grow up, and see this through. She owed him that much. Her mother knew just when to step in and when to let her grow as a woman, and she was grateful for her mother and her wisdom but most of all for her love.

Mary Lou took a huge step toward maturity when she gathered her thoughts about this Bill versus Luke conflict. Germany wasn't the only one being bombed. She'd had a bomb dropped on her heart that destroyed her hopes for the future. As she wrote another letter to Bill, she kept saying to herself, "Just be natural, business as usual."

She was back on track with Bill. Only God knew how this would turn out!

The month of October 1944 brought a drastic change in the social and operational atmosphere of the squadron. Catania placed a ban on liquor purchases and the officers club, and the enlisted men's club closed its doors. The weather continued to hamper the efforts of the pilots and crews. A total of ten missions and 116 sorties were flown against enemy positions in Northern Italy.[14]

While the 310th Group was fighting the Germans, Japan put into operation the kamikaze corps. Kamikaze was a suicide tactic use by the Japanese military to crash aircraft filled with explosives directly into enemy vessels. This corps was influenced by the Bushido code of conduct that focused on bravery and conscience. The effectiveness of this kamikaze effort was limited, however. Of the 1,900 suicide sorties during the battles in Okinawa, only 14 percent were effective.[15]

October 5, 1944
Italy

Dear Mary Lou

Just a note to say that everything is still fine with me and all that sort of thing. How are things around home these days? I'm sorry that I haven't written you in such a long time, but you see I am not at the base right at the present. I'm over here in Italy and all my mail is going back to the base I know that I have some mail from you but the trouble is I'm not there to receive it and don't expect to be for about another month or so, until November I think I don't know for sure. I haven't time to write anyone the last two or three weeks but while things are a little quiet tonight, I thought I would drop you a line. As I said before the mail is not coming in for me so there isn't much, I can write about but at any rate I'll do my best. I don't hardly know what to think about the gang. From the letters I receive I'm told a lot of the girls are married and having babies. It's bad enough that their husbands are transferred overseas without them having babies. What I mean is for one I don't see any point in it, I can't see why they don't wait until the boys come home to stay before they start a family then that way there wouldn't be all that worry. I know if I were going overseas and my wife had a baby, I would be plenty worried about her. When I get a son or daughter, I want to be there to watch them grow up not over here some place. When the boys go home their children will probably be a couple years old and that takes all the fun out of raising children. I want to watch mine grow up to hear him say his first words and see him walk for the first time and all those things. I think you see just what I'm talking about don't you? Oh well that's their life and not mine so it doesn't bother me anyway but I still can't see why they don't use their heads about it.

How is Flora making out these days? The last letter I had from her I answered but I haven't had another one from her that I know of. Maybe I have one at the base now I don't know, when you see her tell her that I said hello and

Ann Cason

will you also all the rest of the old gang. I was hoping once that all the fellows would be home for this Christmas but now, I know that that's out. I think it will be much near next Christmas than this one. I'd like to have the addresses of fellows if you would get them for me. I've asked several people to get them for me, but I guess not any of them have time to do anything like that. I guess that just about takes care of all the girls out there in the community who have married except you doesn't it? I couldn't hardly say that you are in the community now that you are living in town but any way you are still one of the gang.

Say Mary Lou how about that date tonight or maybe I should say how about a date tonight? We can take in a movie and have dinner downtown and from there it will be just a good time. What do you say? What in the world am I talking about, am I going crazy. I must be? I'm not crazy it's just a little wishful thinking that's all. One of these days I'll be home and then oh boy!!!! I don't think you ever did tell me who your boyfriend was that is overseas. What is his name? In the letter that I wrote some time ago I think I mentioned something about it then, the fellow that I named is that right or is it someone I don't know? I think that it is Luke. He is a pretty good guy; I always did like him. There is just something about him that makes a good friend.

I think I told you about Ellie, didn't I? well if I didn't' she is the one and only and lives in Georgia and if I can get back home, I think I'm going to marry her. She is the sweetest girl that I've ever known, and she is everything I ever dreamed for. She is strictly my idea of a wife. I don't know why I'm telling you all this stuff, maybe you are not interested oh well you are a good friend to me, and I know I can tell you about her. I like to tell someone about her in fact I'd like to tell the world about her.

Well you know I think I had better close for this time, but I will write again the first chance that I have. Write often and tell the gang I said hello and all that sort of stuff. See you soon (I hope)

Love Bill

CHAPTER 13

The Future

During November 1944, the 381ˢᵗ Squadron continued bombing activities, totaling twenty-two missions and 195 sorties flown. The missions were primarily against enemy communications in Northern Italy. On two separate missions, the aircraft of the 381ˢᵗ went outside its target area and launched an attack on central enemy communications in Yugoslavia. These targets were heavily defended by antiaircraft guns, but the squadron suffered no aircraft losses. The members of this squadron were awarded one Silver Star; two First Oak Leaf Clusters to the Distinguished Flying Cross, five Distinguished Flying Crosses, one Air Medal, and 222 Oak Leaf Clusters to the Air Medal.[16]

Mary Lou and Bill continued to write each other, with Bill dodging the details of the war and Mary Lou keeping it light and simple with no commitments. Plans were developing for the "first date" when Bill returned.

One letter brought news he thought Ellie was a little jealous. Bill wanted Ellie to understand a deep friendship had formed between them, and he wanted to repay Mary Lou for faithfully writing to him. He thought the best way to do that was a night on the town she would remember forever.

After the first date with Mary Lou, he wanted to make his way to Georgia to see Ellie and return with her to Dolphin Cove to meet his folks and Mary Lou. He then added that maybe Mary Lou and Luke could join them on a double date.

Mary Lou and Bill agreed the right thing to do was to share these plans with Ellie and Luke. It was a safe plan, up until the double date part. Mary Lou was not sure Luke would go along with that. Her single date with Bill would be hard enough to explain.

October 22, 1944 Italy

Dearest Mary Lou,

I'm sorry I haven't had a chance to write you before now. I've been going to school over here in Italy and I haven't much of a chance to do anything, they keep me pretty busy all the time. We have Sundays off and we also have Thursday a half a day.

This is the first time I haven't been to town on Sunday. The reason I'm not today is because I'm on guard tonight and I can't leave the school, I can leave but I don't want to I might not get back in time to go on shift and that in the Army isn't so good. While I have a lot of time on my hands I thought I might try to write some letters. I've made several tries at it but I can't seem to think of anything to say. There really isn't much I can tell you about Italy. It's about the same as it was the last time I was over here. They seem to have a few more facilities for the fellows than they did before but I'd still rather be back in the States. Can you imagine anyone wanting to come home? I don't want to go back home, there is too much excitement for that but don't (I repeat) don't let anyone give me the chance to return, I'd show you just how fast I could come home and I'm not kidding.

Have you seen any of the gang lately? I was wondering how they are and if there has been any change since the last time I received any mail. I had a letter from one of the girls telling me all about her new baby. You know I don't know why all those girls tell me about things like that but it does seem to make news and I do like to know about things like that. How is Flora and her baby making out these days, tell her I said hello will you. Also when you see her tell her I said I haven't had a letter from her husband yet. I bet he's in quite a place if he is stationed on an island down under. I really know how that can be because I've been there and that has been a long time ago. Of course I've been off the base but we were not going to land in enemy territory. This is my second trip and I'm really having myself a time. There is one good thing about Flora's married life, she had quite a bit of time with her husband before he was transferred overseas. When I return to the States I'm getting married and I hope mine is as lucky. They are going to have a rough time trying to get me over here again once I do get home. I think I had rather stay over here for a few more months so when I come home I can stay instead of coming home now and having to go to the Pacific or somewhere else. That isn't good at all.

How about some more pictures of the old home place? The last ones you sent were swell. I have this picture you sent me of yourself in my wallet and some of the fellows are crazy about it. One of the fellows asked me for your address some time ago and I gave it to him. I suppose you will have a letter from him before long.

You know I think I had better close for this time, I have to drop a line home and let them know I'm still kicking and all that sort of stuff. Take it easy and write when you have time

Love, Bill

December 1944 brought little change in the activities of the squadron. Stationed in Corsica, a total of eighteen missions and 147 sorties were flown. Targets for these missions were enemy rail, communications, and supply dumps located in Northern Italy. Expert accuracy by the pilots and crews of the squadron brought seven Distinguished Flying Crosses, three Bronze Star Medals, two Air Medals, and 171 Oak Leaf Clusters to the Air Medal.[17]

December 23, 1944

Dearest Mary Lou,

How are things around home these days? I received your card today and I see you haven't forgotten me. It's really nice of you and I appreciate it a million. You can rest assured I'm thinking of you.

I have a little secret to tell you. Speaking about forgetting you don't think I could because ever since I mentioned you to Ellie, she won't let me. You know I think she might be a little jealous. I told her to forget it because there wasn't anything between you and I except a good friendship that would last always. By the way she wants you to write her, said she would enjoy hearing from my other girlfriend. She's quite a kid though and I'm crazy about her. In fact I'm so crazy about her I think I might marry her when I get home if she will have me. I think I will bring her home with me anyway. Don't worry because I'm coming home first, you remember you and I have a date. You know, I sort of want to make that one my last and I can't think of anyone that I would rather have it with than you. I'm sure Ellie and Luke won't mind too much. Ellie I know wouldn't exactly encourage the idea, but she knows I love her and she loves me and that is what we are building on!!

Well I can't seem to think of anything to write about so I'll close for this time. Write soon and tell all the gang I said hello. See you soon

Love Bill

Taken from the daily log of the Fifth-Seventh Bomb Wing, 310th Group (M), 381st Squadron, it read as follows:

Special Outline Section

During the first month of the New Year, 1945, the squadron, having passed nearly all of the Old Year here at Ghisonaccia, Corsica, became greatly excited about the plans to move to the Adriatic coast of Italy. Prefabricated buildings were torn down, metal scrap was collected, and some equipment was crated, only to have the proposed move postponed for thirty days, if not indefinitely.

Combat operations maintained a steady high level, despite an unusually wintry January for the Mediterranean, with a total of eighteen missions and 166 sorties flown. These operations were again directed against enemy targets in Northern Italy, chiefly rail communications along the vital Brenner Pass supply line ...

A new feature of squadron activities was the beginning of a series of weekly orientation meetings in the enlisted men's mess hall. Surprising capacity crowds turned out to hear two talks by Captain Henry G. Gilliam, our ground liaison officer, on the subjects of the eastern and western fronts, and an expanded program is planned for the future ...

Monday, 1 January 1945

The New Year dawned on a spotless blanket of white snow—our first fall of the season. Now we no longer have to look up the Corsican mountains, which at present are obscured, for a picture of "White Christmas."

A stand-down was called by midmorning to everyone's relief, since this is traditionally the number one "morning after." Interest has been running high in the annual football bowl games in the States.

Meal hours were mercifully extended for the holiday. Breakfast, with fresh eggs and sausage, came from 0730 to 0930, while the festive dinner, featuring turkey and mince pie, was not served until 1430 hours. Only coffee was available for supper, so that the KPs might share in the celebration.

No bombing missions.

Tuesday, 2 January 1945

My Pal Joe was the evening movie feature. Lately, our film schedule has been upset because many of the releases were recalled to Italy.

No bombing missions.[18]

February 11, 1945

Dearest Mary Lou,

Just a line to say hello and that everything is fine with me. How are things around home making out these days. Are you still working or have you finally decided that working is no good for a young lady. I'm only kidding you I know that working will keep your mind off Luke some and you will not worry so much, right? Well you just keep your chin up and it shouldn't be too long before this war is going to end and then all of us will be together again. I don't mean all of us I just mean some of us. I believe that when the fellows come home they are going to take their wives and go to their homes. We'll be together though, you, Luke, me and Ellie and the rest of the gang. The ones that are not married. I know the fellows around there will come back married or not. You know I would like to see that old gang together just once more.. We sure had plenty of fun in the old days didn't we? Those were the days and I'm not kidding

    I'm sorry Mary Lou that I haven't written you in such a long time but honest I've been so busy that I haven't much time to do anything lately. I haven't been writing any one like I should, I know but that is something that

I have no control over whatsoever. I do have a chance to write at night but then its only about one letter and that doesn't leave too much time. I'll get around to writing everyone before long. Before long I'm hoping to see you all and then I will not have to write letters. I do want you to know I appreciate your letters and I want you to continue writing.

The situation looks good over here and I know that if things keep going the way they have, I'll see you before long. I guess we have boys who are in the gang stationed all over the world now. Some of them dead and gone but by far not forgotten. But as you know this is war and someone has to pay the price. None of us were shipped over here for a picnic and I don't want talk about that. Let's forget it for now, okay?

What do you know I received a letter from Flora the other day and she sent me a picture of herself and baby. You know it really did me good to see her again too. Not the way you think but it was good to see her. Do you realize it has been just about three years since I have seen any of you. I'm well on my way to the third year over here, that's the bad part about it. Flora says that everything is fine with her and she is in good health. She wrote a very nice letter, told me all about her baby how much he weighs, he is a nice little fellow and I know how happy she is. I just hope that she continues to be that way. It was good to hear from her and I wish she would write more often.

I hope you don't mind me typing this letter. Rick got it from the signal company and on the way back I made him leave it here so I could write a letter. This is the machine that is going in the radio room I think and if that is the case I'll be able to use it more often.

Mary Lou, well there doesn't seem, to be much else that I can write about except that I'm still in good health and I want to get home just as bad as ever. I guess I'd better close for this time. Write soon and I promise I won't wait so long before writing the next time.

Write soon, Love Bill

March 15, 1945

Dearest Mary Lou

I'm sorry that I haven't written you in such a long time but to tell the truth I just haven't had time. I haven't been on the base for some time now. I've been off on what you might call an advance patrol and I sure haven't had time to write then. Even if I did write at that time there wasn't any place that I could mail a letter. Mail coming was the same way too, I didn't receive any mail for a long time. First I was off at school and didn't get any for a long time then when I went off on this detail it was the same way. Now that I'm back maybe I'll have a little more time. It sure was good to be back this last time because I was beginning to sweat it out a bit. I thought for a while that I wasn't coming back, I almost got transferred out, know what I mean. The night that I did get back the first thing that I did was round up my mail and I had quite a lot. I think I got about a dozen letters from Ellie and you can imagine how happy that made me. She tells me everything is going fine and she is still in good health and all that. Most important is she still loves me. I think I have a wonderful woman there and I'm not fooling. You said something in your last letter about me coming to Dolphin Cove first before I go there. Yes I think I will because I want to get an automobile and go up there. When I get there I want to have some transportation. I don't want to get around taking the bus all the time. When I get to Dolphin Cove I'll see you then and when I get back from Georgia I'll introduce you to Ellie. I still haven't decided whether I'll get married when I get home or wait until after the war. I think I should use some good judgement and wait but I don't know. Maybe I'll let my better judgement get away from me, I don't know just what I will do, I'll have to wait and see.

Yes Mary Lou I do enjoy having a friend like you, I don't think there could be a better one. We seem to understand each other and that's the way it should be too. We'll always be pals, that's the way I like to think of you.

I don't know if I want you to write Ellie or not. you might tell her how nice of a guy I am and all that and that's what I'm afraid of. I've been telling her what a heel I am and do you know I think I have her convinced. I think she believes me. What in the world am I saying.

I don't think that Ellie would mind if we had a date. In fact I know she wouldn't mind at all if she was along, know what I mean. Don't worry about it because you will see me before I get married I'm pretty sure. I want to get to Dolphin Cove first because I'm afraid if I get up there in Georgia I might not come back, I might be tempted to stay there and I won't to have a car there with me.

I remember the party that we had at your house and I'll say that was some party. Flora and I sure did have a good time that night, she seemed to be happy and I know that I was. I don't think that we went to another party that we had more fun. I think that one was tops. Everything has changed a little since then hasn't it. Flora is married now and has a baby, all the other boys are in the service and all the other girls are married. You know this war sure split that old gang up didn't it. We might have another party and it may be good but I don't think there could ever be another one like that one. The conditions will not be the same as they were then, well the next one is going to be good anyway because I'll probably be just getting use to civilized people again. It doesn't make any difference if the boys and girls are married we'll invite them all anyway just to have the gang together again.

Well I think I'll have to close for this time but I'll write again now that I have a little more time to spare. I hope I'll be able to stay on the base this time. Write when you get a chance and I'll do the same. Guess I'll have to drop Flora a line and see what she has to say and how things are going with her these days, See you later..

Love Bill

March 31, 1944

Dear Luke,

Hope this letter finds you healthy and happy. Things round here are starting to buzz with talk and activity about a possible surrender by the Germans. It is going to be a joyous day when that happens. I wish I had kept count of all the letters I have written to the soldiers in this war. All of them seem to appreciate it so much, especially one in particular, Bill. He has written me and asked me for a "first date" when he returns. He said he wanted to repay me with a night on the town. I am sure he means nothing more than that, because he is engaged to a girl in Georgia who is the sister of a good friend,. He also wants the four of us to double date one night. I hope you understand I feel somewhat obligated to see this through and to put to rest any rumors you may have heard about a relationship between me and Bill. We can discuss this further when you get home Love,

Mary Lou

Luke's response to her letter was somewhat surprising. She was a bit confused at his agreement to the first-date situation. His letter read as follows:

> I have to agree with you. I think you should honor your agreement with Bill and keep those plans. You need to fully explore any feelings you might have for him. Your future happiness depends on it. I must now be honest with you. This war has brought new people into our worlds, and mine is no different. She is the daughter of my uncle's best friend, and we have been corresponding for a while now. I know what you must be feeling, and I need to also explore my feelings for her. We will have time, when I return, to fully discuss our plans for the future.
>
> Love, Luke.

Because plans had been made months ago, she felt obligated to honor that request for a first date. She kept telling herself he loved Ellie and was going to marry her. She looked at her engagement ring, and her future flashed before her. She knew she would never be able to replace what her heart knew as pure love, but she somehow had to give Luke a chance. But after reading his letter, she wasn't sure about anything anymore.

CHAPTER 14

It's Over

May 1945 will forever be remembered as victory month in Europe. After nearly six years of war, the Nazi evil had ended. General Alfred Jodi, representing the German government, put pen to paper and signed the act to surrender to the Allies all German personnel still in the field. The fighting was to cease by midnight May 8, 1944. In Norway, 350,000 German soldiers surrendered to the Allies, and the German Army Group South surrendered to the US Third Army in Austria.[19]

Fighting with Japan continued until September 2, 1945. It was aboard the battleship *Missouri* in Tokyo Bay that Foreign Minister Mamoru Shigemitsu and General Yoshijiro Umezo signed the instrument of surrender. On behalf of all the nations at war with Japan, General Douglas MacArthur, Supreme Commander of the Allied forces signed the document, and the war was over.[20]

The end of the war was finally a reality. After a record-breaking number of 399 sorties and forty-two missions, the final mission of the 381st Squadron was flown by only two three-ship pamphlet missions on May 3, 1945, which announced the German surrender to Allied forces, just a day after the Germans surrendered in Italy to Allied forces. This squadron completed two and a half years of combat with a total of 524 missions and 4,368 sorties with only seventeen aircraft lost with an astounding 0.38 percent of planes lost to sorties flown.

In honor of their service, members of the squadron were awarded twenty-two Distinguished Flying crosses, one Oak Leaf Cluster to the

Flying Cross, two Soldier's Medals, sixty-five Air Medals, and 332 Oak Leaf Clusters to the Air Medal.[21]

June 15, 1945

Dearest Mary Lou,

Well, how are you? Surprised to hear from me? I'm sure you are because it has been so long since I've done any writing. I don't think I can explain it either because it's just one of those times I couldn't think of anything to write about..

Yes, I know what you are thinking right now. When am I coming home, well I'll explain all that to you. It doesn't look as if I am, but I know I'll get there before long. All my pals have already gone. Remember Rick he left about a week ago he should be home by this time. I guess I'm coming home with the group from the way it looks. I don't' think it should be but about three months at the most. Once I do get there, I think I'll have a good chance of staying and that is what I'm looking for. If I came back like the rest of the fellows my chances of staying in the Sates after my furlough are very slim. I'm still remembering that date we are going to have when I do get back. I'll be there before long.

Say how is Flora making out these days? Is she still around or just what did happen to her? She wrote me once, I answered here letter but since then I haven't heard from her. I thought maybe because she did not write her husband was back and if that happens to be the case she is forgiven,

Well I'll close for this time. Keep writing until you see me – ok?'

Love Bill

Celebrations were taking place all over the world. The US War Department began computing individual point scores for discharge and redeployment. Bill was finally going home. There was time but for one more letter.

CHAPTER 15

I'm Home

July 18, 1945
Naples Italy

Dearest Mary Lou

I received a nice long letter from you quite some time back but up until now I haven't much time for writing, they had me busy at other things.

I suppose I should tell you that I have been transferred to another outfit and "you guessed it" I'm on my way home. To tell you the truth I can hardly believe it myself, but it's true, I'm on my way now. I can't say just when I'll be there, but it won't be long I know. The boat should be in any day now. I wanted you to know so I wouldn't scare your half to death when I walked in on you. You do want me to walk in on you, don't you? If I didn't write you, when I came home you would get a surprise, oh well we will worry about that when the time comes.

If you happen to see Flora please tell her not to write anymore because. I will not be able to receive it while enroute. I was about due for a letter from her.

I guess there are quite a few boys getting home now and I hope all of them stay when the get there. I don't have any idea of getting a discharge but I'm going to try. I sure have enough points for it, and I know you can imagine how the Army is. Well Mary there isn't much else to write. I'm hoping to see you soon so until I do be good will you. Do not write until I say different – ok?

Love Bill

Bill was transferred to the 340th Bomb Group, 489th Squadron, to be transferred home. He was the last one among his buddies to be sent home. Rick had left two weeks prior to his orders. Bill had one thing on his mind, and that was to get back on US soil. Although he talked in his letters about having his date show him around, he was just kidding. He knew it would take him about two seconds to find his way around Dolphin Cove. After his experiences in the war, he could face anything life could throw at him.

The US War Department had a system called "adjusted service rating score." Service personnel accumulated points that were assigned to different categories. Bill knew he had enough points to qualify for discharge but was holding his breath that his orders did not say "furlough."

Bill received an honorable discharge from the United States Army Air Corps on September 16, 1945. He was officially a civilian and on American soil. Finding his way from Blanding, Florida, where he was discharged, to Dolphin Cove was no problem. He first had to find transportation. Bill bought a shiny, black, 1946 Chevy Stylemaster. He was determined to arrive home in style. His army uniforms had served him well during his enlistment, but it was now time to pack them away and become a civilian again. New clothes and shoes were next on the agenda. Driving a new car, sporting new clothes, a pocket full of money, and on his way home had him on top of the world. His plan to see Mary Lou and then go to Georgia to get Ellie was coming together. However, he still had not heard from Ellie. Maybe it was because of the transfer to the new unit that had his mail mixed up. He wasn't sure, but he decided to proceed with his plans to have a first date with Mary Lou then head to Georgia.

As Mary Lou read the letter, she could hardly contain her excitement. The love she had for him was still there. She had stored it in her heart for months, hoping one day to deny it, but that was not possible now. How was she going to control this without losing Bill? To share with him her true feelings might be too much for him to deal with. As far as she knew, he was still going to marry Ellie. If he could not be her partner through life, she didn't want to lose his friendship. She now understood how Bill felt about Flora. When you loved someone and you gave a piece of your heart to them, you never got it back. And Luke, dear, sweet Luke. Luke made it home before Bill and spent all his free time with Mary Lou. She politely addressed the "first date" thing with him. Although Luke was not happy about this, he knew he had to let her investigate what feelings she might have for Bill. If she did not resolve them, there was no chance for a happy life together.

Luke also had an opportunity to settle his heart with the lady he had been corresponding with. He knew there was no one else for him but Mary Lou. Mary Lou finally came to terms with her feelings about Luke. How would she tell him? Even if she did not marry Bill, the life with Luke was not possible. She pressed Bill's letter to her heart and began to pray. "Dear God, help me have the wisdom and courage to face the truth about my future. If I am to spend my life with Bill, let me know, without a doubt, the direction that will be your perfect will for us. Amen!"

Weeks went by with no word, but she was not worried. God would bring this to a close. She just had to be patient.

Sarah was just about as excited as Mary Lou at the thought of Bill coming home. Mary Lou was returning from lunch when she noticed Sarah had something in her hand with her name on it. It was from Western Union. She and Sarah were jumping and screaming like two little girls on the playground. Bill was not only in the United States, but he had been discharged from the army, and that meant he never had to leave. She knew in her heart he was on his way to Dolphin Cove as fast as he could go.

When Bill arrived in Dolphin Cove, he was in awe of its southern beauty. From the hundred-year-old, moss-covered oak trees and the endless number of azaleas and camellias to the salty sea breeze blowing in from the gulf, he knew he would never leave this place again. It brought a smile to his face and a peace in his heart. He made his way to the new place his dad bought, and they were right in their description. It was sixty acres of the most beautiful land he had ever seen. This property had it all: pastureland, a lake, beautiful oak trees, and a wisteria the size of an oak tree. He could see his own home nestled under a huge oak tree with his children playing beneath it.

The reunion with his parents was filled with laughter, tears, and a table full of good country cooking. Bill rested for a couple of days and then decided it was time to find Mary Lou and take her on that first date he had promised.

CHAPTER 16

The First Date

On September 21, 1945, Bill went to Mary Lou's house, and finding no one home, he left a note on the door. He was in Dolphin Cove as promised and was ready for that first date. He knew she was probably at work because it was midafternoon but wanted to leave her a note just in case they missed each other.

Mary Lou had had a feeling that morning that this would be the day she would see Bill. She wore her favorite dress—the blue one with the blue satin belt—and had her hair styled on her lunch break. It was Friday afternoon, a little before 5:00 p.m., when Bill walked into the store. Mary Lou caught sight of him out of the corner of her eye. She quickly grabbed Sarah and said, "See that man coming toward this office? I'm going to marry that man!"

Mary Lou sat in her chair and pretended to work. As he entered the office, he said to her, "Mary Lou, how about that date?" It took all the angels in heaven to hold her back from jumping into his arms. She looked at the clock, coyly turned her head, and said, "You are late, but I'll go anyway!"

Mary Lou's supervisor and a couple of her coworkers gathered at the door of her office to witness this wonderful reunion. The workday was just about over, and she glanced at her supervisor as if to say, "Can I leave a little early?" With a big smile, her supervisor nodded yes. Bill took her hand, and the first date had begun.

Mary Lou could hardly contain her excitement. Bill was finally home, and she was with him. There was so much on her heart, so much she wanted to tell him, but she knew she had to be patient and wait for the right moment to share her heart. Bill was having a hard time believing he was actually in Dolphin Cove again. All the things he'd talked about in his letters were coming together. When they walked out the door, she caught site of his brand-new, black, shiny car. He looked at her and said, "Sweetheart, we are going to have a wonderful time tonight, and we are going to do it in style." She looked at him and said, laughing, "And I thought you were joking in all those letters. Bill, you are something else."

The first thing on the agenda for that night was dinner. Bill wanted to sit at a table with cloth napkins and cloth table covers. Mary Lou knew just the place; it was one of the hot spots in Dolphin Cove. As they made their way to the restaurant, they passed the San Louie Hotel, and Bill's thoughts drifted back to the fun times he'd had dancing and dining at that beautiful landmark.

Dinner was perfect! The food was delicious, and the conversation was easy and comfortable. The soft lighting and soft music in the restaurant created an atmosphere of peace and calm. Bill tried to tell Mary Lou all the things he could not write her while he was in Europe. As she listened and smiled at his boy like charm, she had to remind herself his heart was with Ellie. Not once during dinner was there mention of Ellie, nor did she mention Luke.

Next on the agenda was dancing at the casino on Dolphin Cove Beach. The trip to Dolphin Cove Beach was amazing. As they made their way across the bay bridge, Bill could see through the rearview mirror. The lights of the city were dissolving behind him, and with the twinkling stars before him, he knew this would be a night to remember.

Mary Lou would pinch herself every so often to make sure she was not dreaming. She looked at him and thought, *He is real, and this has to be the most wonderful night of my life.*

The casino was packed with returning servicemen and their dates dancing and having a good time, so they decided to take that moonlight walk on the beach he had talked about in his letters.

As they walked along the water's edge, Bill was grateful to be home. The salty sea breeze and the cool, white sand confirmed his presence, for there was no place in the world to compare to his hometown. The sound of the waves crashing on the beach in rhythmic fashion and the moon bright enough to see the white foam spray dissolve into the sand caused them to pause and take it all in. Bill pulled her close to him, brought her hand to his lips, gently kissed her delicate fingers, and softly kissed her lips. It all came together at that moment. The confusion was gone, and the search was over. It had been right before him all those years, and he'd never seen it. It was her persistence, her dedication, her constant movement in his direction. Her honesty and integrity to do the right thing, no matter how difficult. It was the soft, sweet scent of her hair, the tenderness in her voice, and the deep love for him expressed in eyes that could draw him in and hold him there forever. How could he have been so blind? The past was truly gone. He was not a prisoner of the past anymore. Nothing mattered now but her! She held his future in her heart. Dare he tell her? Should he try to put into words the completeness he now knew?

She pulled slightly away from him, looked into his eyes, and softly said, "I love you. I have loved you from the first moment I saw you, when we were growing up in Mossy Oak."

He kissed her again, but this time, it was a kiss of surrender, of hope, and of a future.

He was truly home.

It was the custom among the locals to always carry a beach towel in the car just in case they ended up at the beach. They spread their towels over the moonlit sand, sat down, and talked and talked about their love for each other, including how it grew. And between kisses, they planned their future.

They never made it to the casino!

They knew it would not be without difficulties. Their friends and family would not understand the sudden change of emotion and commitment. And how would they explain this to Mary Lou's mother, who knew all along the depth of her daughter's love—even before she did? It didn't matter. Nothing could change the direction of their lives now. It was forever sealed.

The ride home was much different from the ride to the beach. Mary Lou was nestled under his right arm safe and sound in the front seat of that beautiful car. There was a peaceful quietness between the two of them as they drove to her home on Park Street. He tenderly kissed her goodnight and said, "Tonight is the beginning of our lives together. No matter what ups and downs we face, I will always love you!"

It was hard for Mary Lou to let go of Bill because she was afraid she would wake up and this dream would be over.

As Mary Lou entered the house, her mother knew from the look on Mary Lou's face her daughter had found her soul mate. Although she did not believe it was the right choice, she had to believe in her daughter and that her daughter would make the right choice for herself. Mary Lou shared the events of the evening with her mother, and she was forever grateful for her love and support—even if they disagreed.

Sleep for Mary Lou would not come easily that night because her heart was filled with so much joy yet broken at the thought of returning the ring to Luke. How could one person experience the purest joy and the deepest hurt imaginable at the same time?

The dawn of the next morning found Mary Lou in her favorite rocking chair, where she had stayed all night rocking back and forth while trying to put into words her future. She hoped Luke would understand.

Luke and Mary Lou had a standing date every Saturday morning for breakfast, and this morning was no different. She dressed, composed herself, and remember the words of her mother. "Love is fickle. Life is forever, and the decisions we make have consequences. We must be prepared to bear them good or bad."

When Luke walked into the living room of Mary Lou's house, he took one look at her and instantly knew his relationship with her was over. Without speaking one word, tears rolled down her face. She did not have to tell him; his heart broke into a million pieces as she softly cried. He was devastated! He had held onto the hope that Mary Lou would wake up and see the future with him would be strong and solid. He could not accept the fact she *loved* him but was not *in love* with him.

As she removed the engagement ring from her finger and handed it to him, he politely folded her delicate fingers around it and said, "It's yours. Keep it. And may it be a symbol of my love for you." He kissed her forehead, turned around, and walked out of her life.

Mary Lou dropped to her knees and began to pray. "Dear God,

I understand the promises you offer to your children, but I do not understand the process by which they are delivered. Why does one heart have to break to fill another heart with joy?"

Her mother heard her praying and knelt on the floor beside her daughter. She joined her daughter in prayer, asking for hearts to be joined in union of love and forgiveness and for the future to bring a peace and fulfillment of his perfect will for all concerned.

Luke closed the front door behind him and looked into the yard. He was numb. He knew he needed to go to his car, but he could not move. He was not ready to walk away from the only woman he would ever truly love; however, he had no choice. Maybe he could gather enough strength to make it to his car and head for home. That was all he could ask of himself. He was thrust onto a path of his life he did not choose, and there was no way out. His emotions were so drained that if someone had asked for a drink of water, there was not enough "give" left in him to hand it to them. He was about as low as a human could be without being dead. Where would he find the reason to go on? He had loved her all his life. He couldn't think about that now. He just wanted to go home and never come out. Somewhere in the future, he would have to deal with his broken heart. All he wanted to do now was to sleep. Maybe when he woke up this dream would be over and life would return to what he knew as normal.

Three days later, he woke up and realized this was not a dream but reality. His mother brought food and drink for him and sat with him as he slowly untangled his thoughts about what had happened with Mary Lou. He was the counselor and was supposed to have the answers to life's many situations. Nowhere was he taught how to counsel himself when a tragedy occurred. It was the wisdom of his mother that eased his pain and opened the door to a new life. She explained to him that life was about choices and there were no accidents in the life of a child of God. Every event and circumstance had a purpose to grow that individual to maturity. He had two choices: he could allow the life he had with Mary Lou to dominate his future actions and decisions or he could use that experience to comfort another and reach for a deeper, more soul-filling love. Luke was proud to be the son of such a wise woman. She knew how to talk to a man, straight talk and plainspoken, all delivered with the sweetness of a mother's love.

Slowly, the darkness that surrounded him began to lift and disappear. Strangely, he now knew how Bill had probably felt when Flora married Franklin. A moment of sadness washed over him, and he knew he had to forgive them both. One thing for sure was that leaving Dolphin Cove was necessary to find the peace and love he deserved.

Luke found his way to Canton, Texas, where he built his new life. He married a sweet lady who brought to him the kindness and love he offered to others. It was a good life, but he never stopped loving Mary Lou.

As Mary Lou rose to her feet, the sunlight drifted into the room and filled the room with a warm glow! She dried her tears, straightened her clothes, and was now ready to take her place beside Bill. News, good or bad, found its way around the gang with lightning speed. The news about Bill and Mary Lou was unexpected, to say the least, but accepted by all. Flora was happy for them both. She too was now free from the past.

Ellie took it better than Luke. She confessed to Bill that she had found someone else and was moving on with her life.

The Christmas of 1945 was a very special time. They made public their love and commitment and announced their engagement. The wedding was set for June 6, 1946.

It was now time for Mary Lou to meet Bill's extended family members. His grandparents, John and Geneva, were from the old school of life and love. They believed proper introductions should be made before the engagement. This was not going to be easy. Bill was counting on them to be gracious and accepting, no matter when the introductions were made.

On their way to Pine Glades, Bill tried to give Mary Lou as much history as he could about their home there and how it was acquired. She was about to become a member of a very tight family. Affectionately known as "the folks," John and Geneva had nine children, of which Bill's father, Frank, was the oldest. John was the town blacksmith and was truly an artist at his trade. His abilities had brought enough income for the purchase of a sixty-acre tract of land that they nicknamed "Cross the Creek." The location was obvious! Geneva was the boss of the house. Her skill to cook on a woodstove brought friends from all around to enjoy the meats, vegetables, and desserts from the town's finest cook.

Mary Lou's jaw dropped when they drove up to a log cabin that looked like something she had only seen in the movies. Bill explained "the folks" had built this with their own hands. With no running water, no indoor bathroom, and no electricity, she wondered how something with no modern facilities could be so beautiful and livable.

The iron fence built by John decorated the yard and protected Geneva's delicate flowers. The initials "CC" on the gate assured them they were in the right place. The front porch was filled with handcrafted rocking chairs, benches, and end tables. Placed on rocking chairs were red cushions fashioned from flour sacks sewn on a treadle sewing machine. The front door was a solid piece of oak sporting a door handle made of deer antlers and hinges made in the blacksmith's shop.

As they entered the house, Mary Lou was in awe of the simplistic design of this room. It was a very large room divided only by the furniture placement. The front of the room was decorated with furniture made by John. A large sofa and loveseat offered seating in front of the fireplace, while overstuffed chairs made it possible to chat in comfort.

The back half of the room was the kitchen area. A very large wood-burning stove sat in the right corner near the rear door. The wood box was just outside and convenient to retrieve wood for the stove. Dividing the room into two sections was the largest dining table she had ever seen. It was possible to sit twenty people at one time for a meal. And what fun that was! Geneva hosted an engagement party for Mary Lou and Bill, and the table proved its worth. Mary Lou was fast becoming a believer in this lifestyle of no water and no power. She, however, was not a big fan of outdoor toilets.

Geneva came from the kitchen area to greet them both. Big hugs for all relieved their anxiety about proper introductions. Bill told "the folks" of the wedding plans and encouraged them both to make the trip. As usual, Geneva prepared a meal fit for a king. Fried chicken, ham, mashed potatoes, turnip greens, peas, butterbeans, cornbread, biscuits, apple pie, and chocolate cake were placed on the hand-carved oak dining table.

As John said the blessing, Bill noticed he gently took the hand of Geneva and thanked God for their visit and for Mary Lou, who would be the newest member of their family. Such warmth Mary Lou felt was not from the stone fireplace that covered an entire wall of the living room but from the hearts of two people who loved Bill unconditionally and now loved her. This was where Bill got his strength and character. The example set by John and Geneva would one day be passed onto Bill and Mary Lou's children. Somehow, having no power, water, or indoor facilities was not important anymore.

There was one person in the family Bill wanted Mary Lou to spend some time with, and that was his dad's sister, Lula. Lula was a late-in-life baby and was close in age to Bill and Mary Lou. Aunt Lula had a special place in her heart for Bill. Although she never married, she understood the love a woman has for a man. The man she was in love with was injured in the war and refused to allow her to be burdened with a blind husband. He broke up with her in the name of love. She never dated or loved another but served her parents until their deaths. The special place in her heart now had room for two. Mary Lou and Aunt Lula became close as sisters and enjoyed a lifetime of laughter and tears.

The visit to Pine Glades lasted only over the weekend and would be the first of many. It was going to take Mary Lou a little while to adjust to the living conditions, but she was willing to make the adjustment.

Although Bill's presence was enjoyed, Mary Lou missed the letters. They communicated that way for such a long time that she missed his written thoughts and feelings. She requested another letter.

CHAPTER 17

The Wedding

February
15, 1946

Dearest Lou,

You asked me for a letter last night. Now while I'm just sitting around. I thought I would write you one. I don't know though because I haven't used this machine in such a long time that I don't know if I can or not. Anyway, I can make a try, and you will have to overlook all the mistakes, okay?

I have been thinking about last night all day and you know I have just about come to the conclusion that I'm in love with you. Say, did I ever tell that to you? If I didn't, well, I'm telling right now, darling. I'm in love with you and I'm not fooling either. I thought that I was in loved ones, but that is nothing compared with this. I have never in my life had a girl to love me the way you do. There is only one thing that I want to be sure of and that is that you never love anyone else the way you love me. You know, darling, that I could not love anyone the way that I love you. I don't think I could even if I wanted to just as long as I have you and know that you love me, there isn't any girl that I want to love or want to love me.

I sure did not want to leave last night, and I gathered from the way that you acted you did not want me to eave. Each time I see you darling, I love you just a little more if that's possible. Last night I could see forever in your eyes You know Lou, I told you over and over again that you belong to me and one of these days, not long the future, I know that you will be mine. It's getting harder and harder for me to leave when I come down there. When that old 11:00 comes around, I have to start thinking about going home, and honey. It's getting to the stage. it isn't funny anymore. I love you, Lou. You are mine; I am yours. We love each other and that is all that matters.

Lou, I hate to close this, I could go on forever, but I have to get some work done on the old bus if I expect to drive it anymore so I had better close for this time. I'll write you another one. Pretty quick. Okay? Just remember one thing, honey. "I love you with all my heart."

Yours Darling Forever, Bill

Two more letters from Bill were to be received before she became Bill's wife. They were very private, and his love for her was expressed in a way that was only for her to know.

The wedding was coming together nicely. It was to be a small ceremony at the Methodist church in Dolphin Cove. Sarah graciously agreed to be her maid of honor. Bill's best man was his dad. Mary Lou wore a soft, white, satin, floor-length dress. A three-inch, satin-covered belt with a rhinestone belt buckle accented her eighteen-inch waist. The rolled collar cradled her neck as it joined the one hundred rhinestone buttons that closed the front. Her softly curled hair held a small veil whose length rested on her shoulders. Bill wore a soft, black, pin-striped suit with a white shirt and a black satin tie held together with a rhinestone tie tack.

The day of the wedding, Mary Lou's mother was in the bride's room trying to convince her not to marry Bill, while Bill's family was outside offering Bill a large sum of money to walk away. The two families simply could not accept the union of Bill and Mary Lou. Their backgrounds were so opposite that the families could not reconcile the differences a day-to-day life would bring. Bill's grandparents, John and

Geneva, and Aunt Lula, were the only ones who understood their love and commitment.

It was a beautiful church for a wedding. Sunlight filtering through the stained-glass windows brought a rainbow of colors into the sanctuary where two lives would be joined forever. As the organist began to play the "Wedding March," the groom, best man, maid of honor, and preacher took their places at the altar.

When Mary Lou stepped into the light in the aisle to join Bill at the altar, Bill thought he would pass out. She was more beautiful than he could describe. His knees got weak, and he began to sweat. A million things were running through his mind. How, dear God our Father, did he deserve this blessing? His future with this beautiful lady flashed before him. Home, family, and his soul mate were about to become his.

Mary Lou could not move. Her feet were frozen to the floor. She saw Bill and could not believe how handsome he had grown to be. His strength and character beckoned her to join him at the altar. She looked into his eyes and knew he was saying to her, "I will protect you and love you forever." She kept her focus on his eyes and made her way to a lifelong dream.

As the preacher began the ceremony with "Dearly beloved," they looked at each other with eyes of love and commitment. They did not need to repeat the vows the preacher was offering, because their hearts were joined by the bond of love known only from one soul mate to the other. The sound of their voices filled the air like the sweet aroma of southern flowers in the spring as the words "I do" were announced to all creation. They heard nothing until the preacher said, "You may kiss the bride." It was the first kiss of "forever."

As they walked up the aisle toward the door, they knew their love for each other could only be separated by the final call home.

Mary Lou folded the letter to her daughter, placed it in an envelope, and sealed it. It was a good thing she had done.

While gazing out the window, enjoying the memories of a life she had loved, she heard a knock at her door. "Come in. I heard your wife passed away. I knew you would come." Their lives had come full circle. She hoped her daughter would understand.

Epilogue

Mary Lou and Bill were united in marriage June 6, 1946. They had two daughters and enjoyed the blessings of four grandchildren. Mary Lou continued to work at the department store and retired after twenty years to care for Bill during his illness. Bill graduated with honors from college with a degree in science and taught biology at the local high school. Their marriage was not without problems, but it was their deep commitment of love that held them together.

Bill died of lung cancer at age fifty-seven on June 5, 1981. Mary Lou never left his side. Mary Lou spent her remaining years at the Canterberry Hills Retirement Center. She traveled with her daughters, played with her grandchildren, and peacefully passed away in her sleep at age seventy-seven on June 30, 2004.

While packing away the last items of a life filled with surprises, her family discovered that Mary Lou had left for her daughter a letter in the bottom drawer of her nightstand in her room at the nursing home. It explained everything, including the last visit with Luke at the nursing home. But that is another story.

Pictures

Portrait of Mary Lou and Bill.

Mary Lou and Bill standing in yard.

Bibliography

n.d. *57ʰ Bomb Group.* Accessed October 26, 2019. http://57thbombwing. com/381st_History/HistoryOct44.pdf.

n.d. *57ʰ Bomb Group August 1944.* Accessed October 26, 2019. http://57thbombwing.com/381st_History/HistoryAug44.pdf.

n.d. *57ʰ Bomb Group Dec 1944.* Accessed October 26, 2019. http://57thbombwing.com/381st_History/HistoryDec44.pdf.

n.d. *57ʰ Bomb Group History Jan45.* Accessed October 2019. 7thbombwing.com/381st_History/HistoryJan45.pd.

n.d. *57ʰ Bomb Group History May 1945.* Accessed October 26, 2019. http://57thbombwing.com/381st_History/HistoryMay45.pdf.

n.d. *57ʰ Bomb Group History Nov 1944.* Accessed October 26, 2019. http://57thbombwing.com/381st_History/HistoryNov44.pdf.

n.d. *57ʰ Bomb Group History Sept 1944.* Accessed October 26, 2019. http://57thbombwing.com/381st_History/HistorySep44.pdf.

n.d. *57ʰ Bomb Wing Association - 310thBombardment Group History by George Underwood.* Accessed October 26, 2019. www.57thbombwiing381ˢᵗ.com.

n.d. *57ʰ Bomb Wing Association.* Accessed October 26, 2019. www.57thbombwing.com.

n.d. *57th Bomb Wing Associationb.* Accessed October 26, 2019. http://57thbombwing.com381st_History/HistoryOct43.pdf.

n.d. *57thbombwing.* Accessed October 26, 2019. http://57thbombwing.com/381st_History/HistoryNov43.pdf.

n.d. *57thombwingcom.* Accessed October 26, 2019. http://57thbombwing.com/381st_History/HistoryOct43.pdf.

n.d. *D-Day in New Orleans: July 1944.* Accessed October 26, 2019. http://www.invention.si.edu.

2019. *History of War.* October 26. Accessed October 26, 2019. http://www.historyofwar.org/secondworldwar/index.html.

n.d. *History of War.* Accessed October 26, 2019.) http://www.historyofwar.org/secondworldwar/index.html.

1944. *http://57thbombwing.com/381st_History/HistoryJul44.pdf.* July. Accessed October 26, 2019. http://57thbombwing.com/381st_History/HistoryJul44.pdf.

Knapp, Brigadier General Robert D. n.d. "Memo to: All 57th Bomb Wing Personnel." *Memo to all personnel returning to U.S.on leave or furlough.*

n.d. *Menzel Temime Airfield.* Accessed October 26, 2019. https://en.wikipedia.org/wiki/Menzel_Temime_Airfield.

n.d. *Oudna Airfield Wikipedia.* Accessed October 26, 2019. https://en.wikipedia.org/wiki/Oudna_Airfield.

2000. "World War II Day by Day." In *World War II Day by Day,* by Anthony Shaw, 141, 142, 145. New York: Chartwell Books.

Shaw, Antony. 2000. "World War II Day by Day." In *World War II Day by Day,* by Antony Shaw, 141. New York: Chartwell Books.

Shaw, Antony. 2000. "World War II Day by Day." In *World War II Day by Day*, by Antony Shaw, 145. New York: Chartwell Bools.

Shaw, Antony. 2000. "World War II Day by Day." In *World War II Day by Day*, by Anton Shaw, 182-183. New York: Chartwell Books.

Shaw, Antony. 2000. "World War II Day by Day." In *World War II Day by Day*, by Antony Shaw, 185. New York: Chartwell Books.

n.d. *Women Airforce Service Pilots.* Accessed October 26, 2019. https://en.wikipedia.org/wiki/Women_Airforce_Service_Pilots.

Endnotes

[1]   (57thbombwing.com,n.d.)

[2]   (57thbombwing.com,n.d.)

[3]   Knapp n.d.)

[4]   (A. Shaw 2000)pg.141

[5]   A. Shaw 2000)pg.142

[6]   (A. Shaw 2000) pg.142

[7]   (57th Bomb Wing Association - 310th Bombardment Group History by George Underwood n.d.)

[8]   (A. Shaw, World War II Day by Day 2000)pg 145

[9]   9 (A. Shaw, World War II Day by Day 2000)pg. 145

[10]   10 (D-Day in New Orleans: July 1944 n.d.)

[11]   11 (Women Airforce Service Pilots n.d.)

[12]   12 (http://57thbombwing.com/381st_History/HistoryJul44.pdf n.d.)

[13]   13 (57th Bomb Group August 1944 n.d.)

[14]   (57th Bomb Group n.d.)

[15]   (A. Shaw, World War II Day by Day 2000)

[16]   (57th Bomb Group History Nov 1944 n.d.)

[17]   (57th Bomb Group Dec 1944 n.d.)

[18]   (57th Bomb Group History Jan45 n.d.)

[19]   (A. Shaw, World War II Day by Day 2000)pg.182-183

[20]   (A. Shaw, World War II Day by Day 2000)pg.185

[21]   (57th Bomb Group History May 1945 n.d.)

CPSIA information can be obtained
at www.ICGtesting.com
Printed in the USA
LVHW111258260220
648271LV00001B/158